Anthony C. Mazzella was born many years ago but can't specifically remember the incident. New York City was his home but the South Bronx in the '60s was his playground. It was a simple life of sewer-to-sewer stick ball and summers spent in the "country". As Anthony got older, he learned that there is good and bad, God and Satan, and a constant back and forth between them, all existing in the hearts and minds of people. He hopes you learn this too.

Photo credit: Genevieve of The Parlour in Keyport, NJ (World's Spookiest Place)

Anthony C. Mazzella

Building 8

You Know If You've Been There

Austin Macauley Publishers®
London * Cambridge * New York * Sharjah

Ordering Information
Quantity sales: Special discounts are available on quantity purchases by corporations, associations, and others. For details, contact the publisher at the address below.

Publisher's Cataloging-in-Publication data
Mazzella, Anthony C.
Building 8

ISBN 9781638296942 (Paperback)
ISBN 9781638296959 (Audio book)
ISBN 9781638296966 (ePub e-book)

Library of Congress Control Number: 2023918632

www.austinmacauley.com/us

First Published 2024
Austin Macauley Publishers LLC
40 Wall Street, 33rd Floor, Suite 3302
New York, NY 10005 USA

mail-usa@austinmacauley.com
+1 (646) 5125767

Table of Contents

Dialogues **11**

Crumbles *13*

D.R.E.A.M.S. *14*

Essay 1 *16*

Mira *17*

N.I.B.S. *18*

Oy! *19*

Play 1 *20*

Seatcheck *23*

Senor and Chullo *24*

Funny and Satirical **25**

2059 *27*

Bowels *29*

Coolblueice *31*

Gadget! *32*

Holiday *34*

Indian-Taker *36*

Lilly *38*

Orthodoxy *40*

Parking Problems *42*

Radiation *43*

Struggles 45

TomatoI 47

Gates of Hell **49**

Confusion 51

Etc. – Part 1 (A Trilogy) 53

Etc. – Part 2 (A Trilogy) 55

Etc. – Part 3 (A Trilogy) 57

Flesh 59

Gameshow 61

Gates of Hell 63

Locker Room 64

Once in a Lifetime 65

Pasta 66

Pay Your Fare 68

Purity 69

Ragamuffin 70

Slaves 71

The Man with a Plan (?) 72

Worms 73

Red Glare 75

Historical Fiction **77**

Authority 79

Baggit! 81

Changeling 83

Conversion 85

Guilt 87

Papa's Little Boy 89

Republick 91

Surreptitious 93

Training 95

Triangle: Three Angles – One Conclusion 97

The Jesus Chronicles **99**

Faith 101

Choices 103

Family 105

Comfort 107

Journey 109

Grassmere 111

Advice to Clergy **113**

Blintzes 115

Aesculapius 117

Oscar Wilde **119**

Ad Hoc 121

Periwinkle 123

Tiddlywinks 125

Sherlock Ohms **127**

Ohms – The Case of the Missing Otatoe 129

Ohms – The Case of the Crunchies of the Baskerbilles 131

Ohms – The Case of the Wrong Wishy-Washy 133

Philosophy, Morals, And Everything Else **135**

5 = 5 137

Alicewhite 138

Astrid 139

Busy 140

Carpetbaggers 142
Curmudgeon 144
Eclipse 146
Education 148
Epsilon 150
Finale 152
Gnostics 154
Guest 156
Headache 158
Hesti 160
Igloo 161
Imperialis 163
J'accuse 165
Legacy 167
Nereids 169
Oedipus 171
Ogilivia 173
Pearltree 175
Piltdown 176
Polyphemus 177
Purgatory 179
Midway 180
Republicofdos 182
Seaweed 183
Shadow 185
Sine Die 186
Sludge 188

Snowflakes 190

Squid 191

Squirrels 193

Starless 195

Vulgate 197

Wisdom 199

Dialogues

Crumbles

M=man W=woman

W: What is the matter dear?

M: My foot hurts.

W: From what dear?

M: I am not sure. But I think it was from yesterday.

W: You should have said something. So what happened?

M: The Golden Fumbles cookie truck ran over it.

W: I guess that's the way your foot under the Fumbles crumbles!

D.R.E.A.M.S.

Man1: What's the matter?

Man2: I had this horrible nightmare.

Man1: I thought all nightmares were horrible?

Man2: I am not amused. And as I was saying…

Man1: Hmm.

Man2: As I was saying, I had this nightmare about an orange and yellow fish chasing me. Sometimes it would disappear then reappear in front of me.

Man1: Whoa! What did it look like again?

Man2: Well it kinda' looked like the giant fish kites that the Chinese use in their celebrations.

Man1: And THAT is what was chasing you?

Man2: It was just a dream and as a matter of fact, it was my dream and I can dream anything I want. Nobody gave you a hard time about the dream that you had with Fay Wray and King Kong. Especially the part where you were hanging…

Man1: Okay, that's enough. Point taken. Did it ever catch you?

Man2: No! Like all dreams, it just ended with the fish cornering me.

Man1: Well, I can tell you what that means?

Man2: And the Great Mesmo?

Man1: It means never go out with your shoes?

Man2: What!

Man1: That's right. You ran out last night to the Chinese restaurant and left one at home.

Man2: Yeah?

Man1: And what did you eat?

Man2: Oh, no! Fish. No punch line please!

Man1: Sorry. But Fay Wray and King Kong comments deserve a retort.

Man2: Go ahead!

Man1: You left your SOLE at home and it was trying to catch up with you.

Man2 Wise guy! And you?

Man1: Water. I can swim.

Essay 1

The world of the unknown escapes no one or no another. We are constantly striving to find out about tomorrow. We are constantly saying: Only if I knew the lotto numbers. Or: When will I die? And so on and so forth. Unfortunately none of us is equipped to do so. Folks who say they know the future in some sense do. They can tell us that we may or may not be so successful in love or that the dream job is in the future or what we will have for dinner next Tuesday. So, we plan to go out on a blind date. Or that we go back to school or write a better resume or we plan next weeks' meal. Golly gee whiz! They were right. Hmm hmm. For twenty or thirty bucks, any kid on the street can do that with half a brain. In the real world, we call that a hustle. With a storefront and a clean appearance or the kid with sagging pants, it is all the same. Unfortunately, the old saying "Death and Taxes" applies here. Yesterday: that is a fact. When your goldfish swam the last mile: another fact. Thirty seconds ago: the start of this essay and you reading it: another another fact. The past is the only thing we know and the future cannot be extrapolated from it. Death: we know that. How? Because we do! Something that has happened millions and billions of times in the past and thousands of times in the last five minutes. But why do we need to know that? So we can live to 100 and say, "I lived a good life and I am ready."

And who are you to suggest that? Is that what the woman with the gypsy rag on her said or the guy with the jewel in his crown? Yeah right! The bunion on your right big toe can be just as accurate for the price of cold cream. Somebody once said, "Not even I know the place and time." The end of the world is the most commonly thought of as the end of the sentence. As far as I am concerned, when you go, it is the end of the world. When the guy who just graduated college with all those letters after his name, it is the end of his world. When you are just 47 and expect to get to 100 like your great aunt Mildred, it is the end of your world. The physical world called Earth and its environs may still be here but you are gone. That guy was right. What a surprise.

Mira

*Our help is in the Name of the Lord…*Well where is my help? Here I am almost day in and day out. The same old problems or should I not be so cruel. It is not cruel when I am forced to be judge, jury, and official hand holder? I don't know anymore. I feel I am being punished for some obscure sin that I can't even remember? Was it last Christmas when I…I…See! I don't even remember! Aagh!

*Libera me…*Pray for what? I don't even know where to begin. There are so many! Peace of mind? That's ripe! When in doubt, punt. The old standby. Peace of mind? That will never happen to human beings except when they put the coins on our eyes. And then we'll know. The living will still be in the dark. A letter from the other side? I sure would like to see the postage on that!

*Pater…*Father I have sinned. Please forgive me! No, no! Self-pity? Well why not? There I go again! Being selfish again. Father, forgive whoever did wrong for causing this grief! I can't talk like this! I am losing my sanity or what is left. Kind and merciful? Yeah right! I am so sorry!

*Eloi, Eloi…*Have I been abandoned? I must have been. This would not have happened if it were someone else. It never happens to the beautiful people. Just us ugly folk.

*Ad nauseum…*Am I repeating myself? Can I not think straight? Is my mind a circle? No more excuses? Are other folks tired of my voice or my tears? Why am I forced to suffer this burden alone? They are all cowards! I must be strong! I have no choice!

*Pacem in terris…*I must get this strength from somewhere. Inside me? There is nothing left. From the neighbor? From the minister? All words and no substance. From a complete stranger? Perhaps. Hello my child. Yes, I know you. You do. I am your strength and courage. I am a mirror of all things. I am a mirror of you. Blemishes, warts, scars and all the imperfections that make up you, you, and you. I am the strength that lies in all of us. I am a rock. I am the spring eternal. I am your very soul. I am you.

N.I.B.S.

F=Frank J=Jackie

F: Jackie, what is going on?

J: Nothing, Frank.

F: The wife?

J: Okay.

F: Kids?

J: Yep.

F: The car?

J: AAH.

J: Frank, yourself?

F: I don't feel like saying anything. Your talking is too much and I need an aspirin.

J: Buffered?

F: Yep.

J: How many?

F: Two.

J: Later.

F: Yeah, later.

Oy!

M=man W=woman

W: Did you take out the trash?

M: I took out the trash.
Did you do the vash?

W: I did the vash.

M: Did you do my shirts?

W: If I did the vash, I did your shirts.

M: You didn't mix the shirts with the regular stuff?

W: No, I didn't mix the shirts with the other stuff.

M: You know what happens…

W: Never mind that.
Did you go to Schnitz's Bakery to get the blintzes?

M: No, I didn't go to get the blintzes.
When did you supposedly tell me?

W: Vhen you vuz soaking your feet.

M: No vonder I forgot!

Play 1

Time and place: *Wherever or whenever you happen to be at the time.*
Characters: *I don't know yet.*

<u>Act 1:</u> *Here and now!*

Harry:	What's the matter, Gertrude.
Gertrude:	I have a splitting headache.
Harry:	From what? Your busy schedule? Those tea socials must be nerve wracking.
Gertrude:	Cut the crap, Harry. You know I just do more than those things. Like...
Harry:	Yeah, I know. The Ladies this and that...The Emergency Fund for whatever. What is it this week? Poodles who can't afford a haircut or maids who need a new duster?
Gertrude:	I am getting very annoyed with your sarcasm and I...
Harry:	And you what?
Gertrude:	Oh never mind!
Harry:	You see I AM RIGHT!
Gertrude:	About what? Besides, I am getting sick and tired of this same conversation over and over again.
Harry:	Then don't do the same things over and over and over again. It's very simple!
Gertrude:	Unfortunately for you and fortunately for me, I am not a simple person. I am a very complex human being who has chores in life that are there for improving the human condition. You just don't understand things Har!
Harry:	I understand things plenty!

Gertrude:	No, you don't! I am getting quite annoyed with you. Why don't you just accept me for the way I am!
Harry:	I am really trying to. But there are so many more things to life than tea and biscuits.
Gertrude:	Like what?
Harry:	Like daisies…like birds singing…like the ice cream guy with his music…or even going to a movie. Or even a hot dog with mustard instead of some boring little fluff of dough.
Gertrude:	Fluff?
Harry:	FLUFF!
Gertrude:	I'm tired. Goodbye!
Harry:	So much for discourse.

Act 2: *Then and later. Wrapping it almost.*

Harry:	Hello, Gertrude.
Gertrude:	Hello, Harry.
Harry:	And how are we this fine day?
Gertrude:	Okay. But I still don't like the way you mocked me yesterday.
Harry:	I meant no offense. You're a fine individual with wonderful gifts and talents.
Gertrude:	Well it's about time!
Harry:	Are we going to go down that road again, Gertrude?
Gertrude:	That's the main road. That's my road. The way you go is always down the detour and into the ditch or Slobovia! Or some other God-forsaken place!
Harry:	Gertrude…Gertrude…my Gertrude! You constantly amaze and baffle me all at the same time!
Gertrude:	I told you I was a very complex human being.
Harry:	Yes, you did. Yes, you did.
Gertrude:	Oh, by the way Harry, I have to go now.
Harry:	Why? Another meeting with the Humane Society?
Gertrude:	Widows and orphans of uh, uh. I can't quite remember how they were widowed and orphaned but they were! We are going to give each one of them a gift certificate for a months' free meals at the automat. Now, ta-ta Harry.
Harry:	Ta-ta.

Act 3: *Just a moment later.*

Expert 1:	That didn't work either.
Expert 2:	Another miserable failure.
Expert 1:	I wish we could wrap this thing up. Volunteers are expensive to come by.
Expert 2:	Especially when they have to talk the same and look the same.
Expert 1:	She's such a nice old lady. Reminds me a little of my grand'.
Expert 2:	A little like everybody's…huh?
Expert 1:	Yep.
Expert 2:	I suppose little ole' ladies can be crazy since they have so much to offer from their wit and wisdom. And they are old!
Expert 1:	You're right. Maybe we're the ones that should be analyzed.
Expert 2:	How 'bout lunch?
Expert 1:	Crackers and tea?
Expert 2:	We are crazy!

Seatcheck

M=man W=woman

W: Did you do the laundry, dear?

M: Yes, I did my love.

W: Did you mix the colors, sweetums?

M: No, I didn't my secret sweet.

W: Where are the car keys, my bear? Did you check the seat before we left?

M: We would not be in this predicament if we were not talking about interracial laundry!

Senor and Chullo

S=Senor C=Chullo

S: What a great day, Chullo!

C: Yes, Senor.

S: Chullo, where are you?

C: Here, Senor.

S: Where is here? I don't see you.

C: I am here.

S: I am getting unpleased.

C: I am sorry, Senor.

S: Again I ask: Where is here?

C: I am under your shoe, Senor.

S: How did you get there, Chullo?

C: I was not looking where I was going and you were talking to the pretty senorita.

S: I thought I stepped on a piece of gum. You must look where you are going, Chullo.

C: I have many sorrows, Senor.

S: You are forgiven. Now, pick yourself up and let us go.

C: Yes, Senor.

Funny and Satirical

2059

Winston, please pass me the onabulator. Yes, Charles. Thank you, Winston. Sir, would you like your daily cup of fractious juice? Uh, not right now but I could use a demitasse of harbinger coffee. With or without tar bark? I'll try something different today. How 'bout a spring of sand pebble crystals? I think we have run out of them. Alright, then just some fillpot crystals and a drop of binar juice. Very good choice, sir. Here we are. This is very good, Winston. Thank you. Now, to our day. I will need a few more things. Is the zipzator calibrated to my exact specs? Yes it is. I did it yesterday thinking you would need it today. Good job. Let's see. Hmm. Hmm. The exacto-translator, is that set up? Yes Charles, it is. You never cease to amaze me, Winston. How so, sir? There is nothing that I never need that is not ready to go to work. Well, thank you Charles. You have taught me everything you know and therefore, I know your needs and understand your mind. It is as logical as a is to b and ad is to infinitum. I am just a simple person, Winston and you would have figured things out regardless of the complexity of the situation involved. Charles, you are a modest person with immodest talents. We would banter all day, Winston, but time is of the essence and neither one of us is willing to change our ideas. Let us continue with our work and give praise to the greater glory of science. Yes, for science. Now, a few more things. Two pellets of reinforced glibbar. We have that. One ounce of bellicose hardened zipzap. Roger. A two percent solution of mineral extract. Yes. And one potato chip. How simple Winston. A potato chip. Unfortunately, there is a six-month backlog of potato chips. For what reason, Winston? Apparently, there have been great thefts of already made potato chips from the factories where they are produced only when they are needed. And there has been no need, except for scientific study. Hmm. How distressful! How about a piece of glibbar? I am not sure but it is all we have so let's use it. Fine. Turn on the onabulator and set it for six point one ingles and let it run. Just think, Winston. We may be witnessing a great scientific breakthrough today. A situation that has plagued mankind since the dawn of history, The answer to the ultimate question that may have the final answer today. Listen to that, Winston. A low humming sound but with loud results. Yes, Charles a great day. A great day for science. Okay, it is done! Place it in the cage that is set up. Turn on the monitors so that we may record history at its finest. Here we go, Interesting. Interesting. Very interesting. Oh, no! I fear another failure. Back to the drawing board. Yes, the mouse just crawled right by it.

Bowels

Mirror, mirror on the wall...Already! I get the idea. Now what do you want? You know, you are not with the program. You are to let me go through with the whole "Mirror, mirror" thing and then you are to say...Let's be innovative and try something new and wonderful. Like, "Hi! What's up?" Perhaps even, "It's good to see you." But Noooooo! That darn same ole, same ole. Keep up with the world. Stop being old fashioned. Let the guys down at the union hall see that you are smart, innovative and up to date. How dare you challenge the basic tenets of our business! I do what have to do and you do what you have to do. That's just the way it is! Now, let's get on with it shall we? We shall not! Besides, I got a call yesterday from some young thing of 492 who thinks I am hip and would be fun to spend some time staring at. She is very liberal when it comes to some things, especially keeping up with trends and modern innovation. So, why don't you go and cook up witches brew for I need to freshen up. So I'll see you, I mean, see me later. I knew hunting in antique shops for good help was a bad choice. Reminds me of Aunt Bertha. She had such a good reflection of herself that when she passed, the old dear willed it to an old age restoration shop and let it enjoy a nice retirement of varnish and daily glass cleaning. Makes me very envious. Well, look who the antique dealer drugged in. And how are we? Please don't ask. You're a bit dull around the edges. No glaring moments? Ha! Okay. Okay. First dates are often rocky. You know these things. I wouldn't. I have been out of the market for quite a long time. About 312 years? I think my memory serves me correctly. Yes. That's it. I recall that I met this very engaging and clear looking fellow who was down on his luck. All ready to be tossed into the rubbish pile and whose owner was willing to PAY somebody to get it out of his shop. All I heard was thank you upon thank you upon thank you. Everything went well and it continued that way until just recently when he gazed the other way and found himself to be perfect: no cracks, scratches, or deep etchings. And so he went. And so this shiny creature thought he could do better. I know who you went to see! My great niece Esmeralda. A tramp as far as the reflection can see. One-night stands of ego soothing and shattering moments. I see a small crack around your forehead. You're lucky. All the others were splintered into thousands of pieces. Point taken. I see it is late evening. Anything I can do, my lady? You know. You know. Okay. Okay. Mirror, mirror on the wall, who is the fairest of them all? Why you, my lady. That's better. The glass is never less streakier on the other side!

Coolblueice

That is mighty refreshing, Griswold. Why thank you, Huber. A secret recipe handed down from generation to generation of the Zinkle family. I bet they were a fun bunch of people, too. They were and still are, if I don't say so myself. On occasion you seem a bit stuffy but for the most part, lively. Well, if that' isn't a bit of assurance, Huber! So, what's on tap for today? I reckon I will trek down to the gully and get myself some old and worn-out tires and make them new again. That sounds like some business but how come I never see anybody at your shop, Gris? It's a specialized market that takes the bad stuff and makes it good. Yeah? Yeah! For example, you see that tire over, the blue one? Yes, but why blue? Why be the same when you can be different. I clean them up, patch here and there, and give a fresh coat of rubber with a blue sparkle shine. But I never see any blue tires around. Like I said, it's SPECIALIZED! Oh, I see! Folks like the mundane and boring. But why be different with a blue tire? When you get a cut on your finger, Huber, what do you do? I clean it up and put a band aid on. Okay. Would it be a rubber band aid? Yes, but...Yes nothing! It heals and we go on to the next bruise, and the next one, and so forth and so on. The problem with folks nowadays is the feeling of invincibility and sameness. We all have to have the "I" whatever or the same tattoo or all go to the same spa. All the same. All the black and white. All the everything. Be different. Be unique. Be the one to think out the box. Think of things and I pardon the expression, out of the blue, Huber. Point taken Griswold. Oh by the way, your next project Gris my old boy? Well, I don't know yet, but you kinda' look a little pale. I got some orange paint...I gotta go Griswold. Huh? Where? Joe's Hardware for some invisible paint thinner! Wiseacre!

Gadget!

What you got there, Griswold? It's an uh, um, well I don't rightly know what this thingamabob is. I just invented it this morning in the Little Shop of Inventions and Discoveries. Little Shop of what? The Little Shop of Inventions and Discoveries – the name of my invention factory in the basement. Sounds like the wife got angry at you again and locked you in there. Ah…yeah! What ya goin' to do? Well, be that as it may…it provides a certain amount of relief to me and gives me a chance to exercise the old noodle. From last I can tell the time I was in your basement the place was full of old newspapers, magazines, and a large yet organized pile of junk. Junk? That's correct! Look at Edison. He used junk and look what it got us. From what I can tell just higher electric bills. Ah you have no imagination. I do. When I am on the golf course I imagine myself the greatest golfer on the circuit and surrounding myself with trophies and cute golf groupies. Instead, it takes me ten shots to the hole, a bird that I knocked out of the sky and an 80-year-old geezer wanting to know if I am done yet. So, don't tell me I have no imagination. You do, but it is geared to unrealistic goals and ideals whereas I realize that achieved goals may be smaller and more attainable. At as with time, they can be seen as building blocks toward something more realistic and who knows, that perfect hole in one or at least not taking all day to get the little white ball you hit into a hole. Well I like doing that. Okay, suit yourself if you like doing that. Personally, I like to meditate and contemplate the meaning of life – if there is one. It seems more to me that you like sitting like a pretzel and be a drain on society. I wish you would stop saying that. You are jealous because I received a large inheritance from my grandmother and it allows me to be relaxed and not worry about the hustle and bustle of daily life. Besides, Joan likes it that way because it lets us do things that people can only do when they retire as opposed to doing it when they want to. You act like this is Nirvana or at least, a country club. NO! First of all, I am not a snob and I don't like country clubs. You're the one up before the sun is hitting a little white ball around in the blazing sun and trying to get noticed by the Chancellor of the Exchequer or the Grand Poobah or whatever the 20-syllable title of the Most Important Visitor of the day is. Hmm. I won't get angry at you but in a strange sense you are right. We get a little away from the basics of life and the simple pleasures – such as when the wife and I took little walks or a sip of wine at night instead of me falling asleep with drool at six in the evening. Even when we were dating, walking in the park or lying around the fountain watching the kids play Frisbee or chasing their dog or little sister. See, my little invention worked. But just wait for the next one! It will be a doozy!

Holiday

You know Woodrow, this job is really tiring. I can understand all you're going through Milton. I can't believe you would take a job that is so stressful. I always thought you would enjoy a more relaxing type of existence, such as beekeeper or chief accountant, I mean, VP in charge of accounting. You better correct that! You know who would not take it so kindly with such a slip of the lip! You know who already knows and has a great sense of humor about things. I suppose you're right! A person in his position has to. For instance, you Woody my best pal and great mahjong player is great at what you do. Well, I forget. What is it you do? Don't be a wise ass – oops donkey! You better correct that. Why should I? I'll get fired? That is very unlikely. Who would take over this job? How many do you see making noise to replace me? Not many. As a matter of fact, NONE! ZIP! ZERO! NADA! Sitting in this cramped little cubicle with a filing cabinet and Rolodex. With a rusty little pencil sharpener and knobby pencil, checking this, erasing that, wishing I didn't have to erase that. The erasing part – that's is the worst part of the job. Unfortunately, that's the way it goes and orders are orders. Besides, erasing is done for a reason. But Woody, I am just busting chops. It is the only fun I have in my existence. I know Milton. Just having fun! It's too tense. NO days off. NO sick time. NO vacation time. Remember Milty, we signed up for it and so it is. Hey, Woodrow…WOW! I have just been sent a note in my mail that says I can take some time off. How long? It doesn't say. Who is going to take your place? It doesn't say and I won't ask. Here I go! Okay Milton, have a great time and please send a postcard! You're dopey! Let us see here. Oh, this looks good. A warm tropical paradise, I mean place. I almost forgot what everything looks like, being so wrapped up in day-to-day business. Woody was right. TENSE! TENSE! TENSE! I prefer RELAX! RELAX! RELAX! Now, that is more like it. This sand is so warm and comfortable. The palm trees are just swaying in the wind. The pretty tropical girls. The children building castles. There is so much here. My senses are so alive! Everything is just so perfect!

Here's a newspaper. A murder. A stabbing. People on food lines. Children starving for want of a piece of bread or rice. Maybe I do have it good. I don't know. But, this whole place was designed that way and who am I to change or modify it. Alright. A radio. Let's listen in. "For a record. third month, women at the County Medical Center who have been in labor have still not delivered, as reported by the hospital spokesman. The reported health of the mothers and their unborn children are perfect. They just seem to be in some kind of suspended animation. With little or no pain, they are quite comfortable and becoming quite anxious, but otherwise, okay." Hmm. A newspaper. What have me got here? "Farmers reporting a disaster for their crops. Seeds were planted in the current growing season and have yet to sprout. The last time this happened was 12 years ago when a short burst of locust took place, destroying everything in their wake. However, the local growing association reports no such issue this time." Alright. Everything is becoming quite clear. No seeds. No food! Starvation! Oh man! I would be contributing to all that is hurtful and painful in this world. Back to work! Welcome home, Milton. Glad to be back Woodrow. The finest at whatever you do! A little of this. A little of that! But I sure make a great secret agent and good-looking messenger! The modesty is overwhelming. I know. Now, how 'bout some babies and cereal for them to eat!

Indian-Taker

WASSSS UP kemosabe! Wuz up! Wuz up! Can't you think of any other expressions to use or is that all you learned when you were expelled from the 9th grade? For your informacion, I managed to get to the 10th grade. One day doesn't count. You know that and I know that, but no one else does. You and your parole officer. Ah, com' on. That was many moons ago. Here we go with the Native American phase again. What do you mean phase? Well, let's see. Two weeks ago you were Scandinavian because you got interested in some foreign language film that had a starlet that spoke that language and busied herself milking cows and cleaning latrines. Not cows, moose. Moose? Yes, moose! That lasted a couple days until you went to the new pizzeria on 3rd and Main. And let me guess. I became a pizza maker with a great twist on the English language? No! You thought you were some grand opera singer and nearly got us arrested for breaking Mrs. Wilson's glass flower vase! We didn't, so there! Yeah! And now, you are Chief Dull Blade. Right? Wrong-o! I am a symbol of oppression of the white man from Europe who brought over his many diseases, nasty vermin, an ungodly religion, and assorted other despicable things too ugly to even mention. But that still doesn't answer how you became this victim. Wait a minute! I got it! You were spying on me while I was watching a John Wayne festival on TV! Right? Absolutely not! I have always felt a tendency and a kinship for the oppressed and the downtrodden. Okay. Let me put on some classical music. You don't like classical music. I need to hear it so I can pretend to be a sad and rolling up and down violinist. I am not amused. What are you now? Are you going to shave your legs and become the late Queen Victoria of England? You do look kinda' peeked. Perhaps you should sit on the throne for a few minutes and read about Halloween so I can get the headless horseman to take your head and smash it. You are a very cruel human being. Me? Yes you! How so young Fat in the Head? I am going to let that go and proceed with my explanation. We are human beings and we belong to the universal we. One day we are a turtle, the next a pea pod. The following week we may be a meteor across the sky or a lemming going off the cliff. It changes day-to-day or moment-to-moment. Like a chameleon O' Pain-in-the-Rump? I'm going to ignore your childish remarks and agree with you 100%. In case you haven't noticed you have changed appearance and tone. You remind me of a people long ago in China who went with whoever got them their daily meals. They were called "Rice Christians". If the Communists got them their ration of rice, the people would root for the Commies. If the Christian missionaries did the same, they would rah-rah for God. All this would change at the whim of wind or a bomb. Eventually they were swallowed up by Mao and were forced to adore Mao and his little red book. Eventually as time went on, they got hand fed by the Reds and became willing servants of the Commies, enjoying the fruits of their workers' paradise or heaven on earth. They became so engulfed that they lost their way and under threats of purge and death became the masters of their family and friends so they could get an extra helping of rice and a piece of stale bread. Eventually, through a slow and carefully laid out osmosis planned out in the pagodas of power, they too became swallowed up and wound up like their fellow brethren whom they sold out previously. But some realized what was going on but it was too, too late. They were persecuted and flogged and beaten till they were a massive heap of even and bloodied flesh. They rose again and were knocked back again. Persistent, as in Tienanmen Square, somebody had the audacity to be only one person – themselves. That one lone person or it doesn't have to be just one person. It can be two, three, four or even four-thousand who stand up and say, "Yes. It is we!" We must resist the false people and their false notions and their false gods and their uneven dictates. We are not dead. But we feel as though we are the walking dead. But, no, it is not us! Those who lead these false lies are dead. Let the dead bury the dead. They will consume themselves in nonsense under the heavy shovel of hypocrisy beating on their heads until they are trampled into the ground of retribution and shame. Be yourself and no one else. If you must die, die standing up for your principles and say, "Yes. I am not ashamed but proud of my uniqueness. I am I and no one else is." Where are you now going? I thought I'd go over to Tom's house. A barbecue? No. He's showing old World War II films. Wonderful! He'll come back with a mustache, a bowler hat, and cigar!

Lilly

See the lilies of the field. They do not toil yet the Heavenly Father cares for them. There is a season for all things. Turn turn turn! He that troubleth their own house shall inherit the wind. Seems like a severe case of indigestion to me. You're not acting serious. Oh, yes, I am. Now stop your nonsense! Pick out what you want to talk about so we can plan the town's azalea festival. That's rich. Azaleas in the middle of a God forsaken desert. God has not abandoned a desert for he put it here. Why? To amuse himself at two humans who haven't got a shred of dignity nor at least, a half-broken air conditioner. Why do you talk like that? Because I like hearing the sound of my own voice so I don't go crazy on half eaten crackers and stale cheese sandwiches. They are only stale because you leave them out while you are drooling with one eye open and the other at half-mast. Now, don't bring Jonah into this. I wasn't but since you...Argh!...Enough already! Let's see...There was a tax collector named, uh... I can't even remember his name. Was...is...no, it was Raoul... This is not Don Quixote and enough of your heretical meanderings. I was not being heretical but simply trying to counteract your seriousness in the matter of cheese and crackers. By the way, that is my privilege to discuss cheese and crackers and whatever else is dry and stale including present company. The only thing stale in this place is your lack of wit and good table matters. Specifically, removing various parts of your days' meals from your teeth while complaining and incorrectly so, about my cologne. That is for sissies and Baptists. Real men use brittle soap and ice-cold water and a good smoke of Habaneros 32. God, I miss those quiet times back when we were really alive and had a good 32. Better than 24 but not as expensive as a 49. Such is the fate of forsaken men and schoolgirls after the prom. You went to a prom at least sometime in your miserable little existence. Of course I did! I bet you smelled as sweet as a tiger lily and as miserable as a caged frog. NO SMARTASS! I smelled like musk: strong, virile, and...like you hadn't bathed in months? No and at least I wash on a regular basis. Well, smarty pants I bathe on a regular basis – whenever I regularly please thank you very much! This is not working out too good. Why do you say that? The bickering, the back and forth, the snide remarks, cheese and crackers. How did that get in? I don't know but it is amusing nonetheless. But it will all come out in the wash. You mean a bath? Now don't start or you will be on the list with your ex. Okay you win.

Orthodoxy

What's the problem now? No problem. Why do you ask? You have that look on your face. Oh! You mean "that look"? What is "that look"? A little wrinkled around the eyebrow and a slight twitching of your right eye. I see my friend. Stop being funny. So, what is the problem? Well, a pickle of one. And that is? If I knew what it was I would be trying to resolve another. Your usually double-talk and gobbledygook are getting a little stale. Like you always reminding me about it? Exactly. Tit and tat and cat and mouse. I always like the one that you only use once in a while. What is it? Ham and cheese. You're right. Another one of my ways of describing your eccentricity with words and looks. Might I remind you "ham and cheese" go together as opposing each other. It's my saying and it means what I what it means. Sooooo, wiggle your eyebrow and I'll go "ham and cheese". Alright? Not alright but I don't have time for further word battles or ancient food sayings. Now that you have wasted some more of my precious time see if you can be productive in helping me with my current dilemma. Okay boss! Let's see. Oh, here we are back. Where is my slide rule? Did you take my slide rule? No. Why would I take that dinosaur from you? You're both about the same age. I am not amused. Are you going to help me or what? Alright. Alright! Now, where is that blasted slide rule? I don't know. I guess paper and pencil will have to do. Be a good little lab assistant and sharpen this pencil. Do it before I crush you mealy brained brain between thumb and forefinger so scat! Hmm. Hmm. Hmm. Ah, yes. Yes! Just one more calculation but where is my pencil. You! Get over here now! Sorry boss. The pencil broke. How did you manage to take a simple project and turn it into a molehill? Skill! That's enough of your put-zing around. I only took you services because I lost a bet with the Ganymede project head. Now get over here. Let us try to remember what is in our arsenal of thought hand grenades. Tick tock tick tock the mouse ran up the clock. Ring. Ring Rung. Rungs? Rungs! That is it oh incompetent one! Rungs! Don't you see? Of course not! You are a mental midget, my mealy mouth helper. Rungs. That is it! Go to room I think 3A in section 5. Tell Woodrow I want the green box with the label with Z's name on it? What? Just go man go! Just go now! I'll call ahead because I am sure you'll go to the lab with the experimental purple mice instead. Rungs! Tick tock! The purple mouse ran up the clock. The clock struck 12 and the mouse turned into a pumpkin, I think. Never quite could remember. Oh, you're back good! The right box. Even better. There it is! The answer to all answers I am looking for! All I see is a blank piece of paper. Of course! You are a dim bulb. The answer is clear. It sure looks clear to me. Be quiet! Well, there is the answer. Oh! Not oh! But a...! A WHAT! AN ANSWER! To what? To anything you want. Fill in the blank! With what? Anything you want! Ask me a question. Okay. Two plus two equal what? Three. Three? Three. The answer is in front of you. It can be anything you want. Stop sticking to basic ideals and expand your mind. Another question this time for you. The moon is? Square. That's right! It's right because you thought about, analyzed it, and pronounced it! As long as you went through a couple of simple steps to come up with the answer, it's right. The caveat is though, if it is a fact of nature or otherwise fixed set of principles, this premise of mine is incorrect but logically thought out. And logic is the key. Being stuffy is for Teddy bears and plush dolls. Wake up! Try something different than old worn-out principles and discovery of realms will be yours! Wow. Now I'm hungry so just get me an old-fashioned bacon, lettuce and tomato and hold the pickle. Pronto!

Parking Problems

Hello honey, I'm home! How was your day? Exhausting as usual. These four-hour days are brutal. I know. I know. Oh by the way. Yes, dear? What is the car doing on the fire escape? Don't ask. The crane man was so busy today. More so? Yes! Not only the usual stuff but this being the summer, more tour buses got themselves snagged up into the Wordberry Building. Couldn't they just wait their turn? Unfortunately not. You see, 200 Japanese tourists and 89 Buddhist monks were caught up and...So? Sushi, chanting and being 50 stories up doesn't mix with being upside down. I guess I should be thankful for pigeons. So, what is for dinner? Squab.

Radiation

Are you keeping an eye out? What? ARE YOU KEEPING AN EYE OUT? Nothing by my house. I am not worrying about YOUR house. Your house is a block away. I know that my house is a block away but remember – any direction is possible. Remember the laws of nature and improbability…I am not a lawyer but a poor schnook like you trying to survive the wrath of this horrible plague upon mankind. Okay, you win. THERE IS NOTHING NEAR US and I just glanced toward where I live and it kinda' looks like nothing there, I think. Thank you very much. It's about time you got with the program and if there's time, we'll go over to your house, if we survive here. You mean if you survive. What do you mean by if "you" survive as opposed to us? I can always get up, leave and let you manage on your own. Just because we have been bosom buddies that doesn't mean I have to share your demise. After all, I have to worry about my own future and besides, when your problem erupts, I doubt you will even be able to help. You're right. I shouldn't be selfish. Just thinking about myself. If you want to leave now go ahead. I understand. Apology accepted. I will go almost down with your ship and then I'll flee to my own lifeboat and row to my own leaky vessel. That's fair enough. In the long run we are all in this same whirlpool together. You got any beer left in this place? Yeah. There's some in the fridge or if it's not there, check behind the couch. Behind the couch? That should have been my first guess. And look what else I found! Do you prefer pepperoni, anchovies, or green? Or green what? Well, let me say this. If you want some medicine, the green stuff is for you. Or you might want to keep it around for later for when you need it. Sad, but true. Sad but true. Ah well. Now back to our show! Nothing on the horizon. That's surprising. I was led to believe it would be around this time but that's okay – it gives us more time to prepare. You ain't kidding! So…How are you feeling about this? At first it didn't faze me too much. I feel I have built up a good immunity toward this kinda' thing. But, I suppose nothing is ever one-hundred percent. You do whatever you can, but like I said before – improbability and the element of surprise can never ever be trifled with or understood. Just dealt with. You are a better man than I. I was never built to accomplish or understand this. I guess I am one of God's more passive and less resistant creatures. Good in some, bad in others. I am tired of my traits and wish I was of better stock. This plague, this problem has roamed the land since time immortal. I don't know. I just don't know. Wait a sec! There's a light. It is distant but it is a light! Getting closer. Getting closer. It's now on us! God help us! This is where I leave. I gotcha'. Thanks for the shoulder. Bon voyage mon ami! Sail thee well! The light – it's here! Oh God! This is torment! Now I know how Poe felt! Anything to be a raven! I feel the heat, the sensation, the chills up and down my spine! The light is now shining in! It's off but, but…Honey, I'm home!

Struggles

Rollem! There's poor Tara running to the top of the building! OH NO! What is she going to do? No love is worth it Tara. Really! Get back inside! She's on the ledge and she's...she's...going to jump! The humanity of it all! Ah!... There she goes! Falling down like a child's rag doll! Bouncing off of the side of the building...Arms flailing...Legs flaying...Like a jumping jack that's not jumping! Tara just hit the hard sidewalk where many a feet have trodden. Oh look! There's her eyeball. I think...I think...that's her right one. Tara had just seen an ophthalmologist and it was giving her trouble anyway. Here comes the press! No long exposures here. Tomorrow's headline captured right here in our very eyes! Where is the ambulance? Nothing! This poor girl is going to die if...Wait! Here comes the doctor! Hooray for Tara! Hooray for the world! The doctor is taking something out of his bag...Good...Good...Good...That thing he is taking out of his bag...It's a...No!...Not that! That is used on animals when he has to check their a...! Sorry for the profanity. I do go to services every Sunday so don't you worry. Now back to Tara. That man is a vet. A vet! Tara is not a horse or cow. I suppose though when in a pinch any kind of doctor will do. That reminds me of my pet Francis the cow who needs... Nevertheless... Look at that! Miracles upon miracles. Heavenly intervention has occurred here in our very midst! He just put her eye back in and now she is moving! The crowd is cheering! The press has gone crazy over this. Each photog sees a Pulitzer in his future. Each clamoring to get to the front of the line. The police are here! Tara is being escorted to the ambulance but she refuses. What is she saying? Just a bruise...A little mascara running...a warm bath...will find a new boyfriend...can see better...thought the doc was cute...has the magic touch... Tara is a real trooper. There she goes. She hops in a cab as though she was just coming home from work or shopping. Bless her soul! Here's the doctor. A real miracle worker. You did a magnificent job. Well thank you, Walter. And your name? Arugula. No, not your dinner...That is my name. It is Dr. Vito Arugula. In my view, all pains and aches are the same in humans as they are in other animals. Some bird seed here…A horse pill here. A little magnesia for poor puppy who just ate a tennis ball. In some cases, this thing. What is that, Doc! It is what we call in the trade a happy stick. A what? A happy stick. I see. It works like a plunger and we…I think our audience gets the drift. Well…Walter, you look a little cheeky how 'bout a peek? NO! I used it on the poor girl to remove the bad humors and used it in reverse to give her the sight of both eyes, Amazing! Not bad for a miracle worker. Well thank you Dr. Arugula and enjoy your salad tonight! My pleasure. An extremely emotional day here in midtown. The ups and downs – literally – of a love crazed girl driven to desperation only to be saved by a doctor whose specialty is plumbing in animals. This is your news worthy correspondent Walter Beluga. Cut! That's a take. Put it in the can! Send it over to Zinger's Pharmacy and Sweet Shop. Tell him I'll give him an extra twenty if he has it by dinner time. Roger!

Oh Mr. Zartz, I have some bad news for you. Yes, Hugo? It seems that somebody has beat you to the punch. What punch? Apparently, somebody got their film from Zinger's just before you dropped of yours. You mean…mean… Alf…yes. That is the umpteenth time he has beat me. He is extremely jealous just because I use a redhead instead of a blond. And a REAL redhead. Not someone out of the bottle. I…I…feel sick. Huuuuug…Oh Johnnie? Yes Hugo? Get the vet and his plunger. Tell him it's about the size of a football.

TomatoI

(I don't want to offend vegetarians or word aficionados – author)

Are you ready to order or shall I give you another 20 years? My dear Prudence, the waitress deluxe, the hostess with the mostess, the woman with the dexterity of a brain surgeon, the...You know Fred, the longer your nonsense is only matched by the shortness of your tip. Dearest P., you flatter me more and more each time and...As I said, you give me a less and less tip so that means I will have to endure your "compliments" for at least until the next age. By the way, F, it's freezing outside so cut the crap, order your food, and give me more than a plug nickel so I can at least get a scarf before I become a bunch of rocks or oil. Your eloquence is well taken so please my dear Prudence I would like to try something different tonight. Instead of ordering a burger deluxe with fries, lettuce, crisp pickle and no tomato – by the way which shows up anyway and don't tell me you don't recycle it – try this. A burger deluxe with you holding the burger, holding the fries, holding the lettuce, holding the pickle. Period. Pickle? NO, you dumb luscious thing, I SAID PERIOD! Oh! Fred, period. Now that you have figured that brain twister and unknotted that pretty little red hair of yours, tell me pray tell what is left of my evening's repast request. Hmm. Hmm. Uh, let's see, Uh oh ho. Oh yeah, yeah. I got it, I think. The bun, the burger bun. Prudence, you ninny. The TOMATO! Of course! Fred that was what I meant to say. Hey, does that mean you give me a decent tip tonight. Absolutely Prudence! So where is it Fred? Last time I checked in the Miss Manners world is that you serve me the food, I eat it, and if I don't suffer from convulsions after I suffer from repulsions, you get your just desserts. You want dessert Fred? We got a great cream pie. How 'bout that? Or...My sweet thing! Just a play on words. Please...my love a tomato! Hurry up Miss Prudence! To the kitchen! Make haste! Make haste! Poor girl! I overwhelmed her with a simple request! I feel I have caused irrevocable damage to her pretty little head and may cause her freckles to multiply and make her look like my overripe dinner. Oh well. Ah! HERE YOU ARE! My dear lovely, you have successfully completed your mission. A new record for this dubious establishment and its lovely hostess. I barely had enough time to run across the lane and get my usual embibement of tea with a nip of medicinal alcohol for the slight cold that inhabits my liver. This fruity red thing looks scrumptious and meaty as red as the hair on your beautiful cranium. However, I have lost my appetite for this but have gained another. You're kidding? Right Fred? Right? Wrong my gem of a stone. It is true I had no stomach for just this tomato but in reality for my usual well-done animal on a bun. At least you can give me a better tip than you usually do Fred for wasting my time on a whim by a lunatical old geezer who doesn't appreciate my value. My dear Pru I do I do. Here is your tip: not in coin terms but in terms of life and the importance of living as opposed to existing and worrying about a silly scarf or the value of one's bankbook. It is this: we too often overlook the little things in life and yes, the lowly tomato is one of them, especially when it is part of a salad or a burger. The value of ones' self is what we place on it. Whether it be a tomato or a crouton or a lovely little waitress. Come Prudence, let's go home. It is getting late – the children will be waiting for us. Just as we have for the last 20 years? Yes, my love, for the last 20 years!

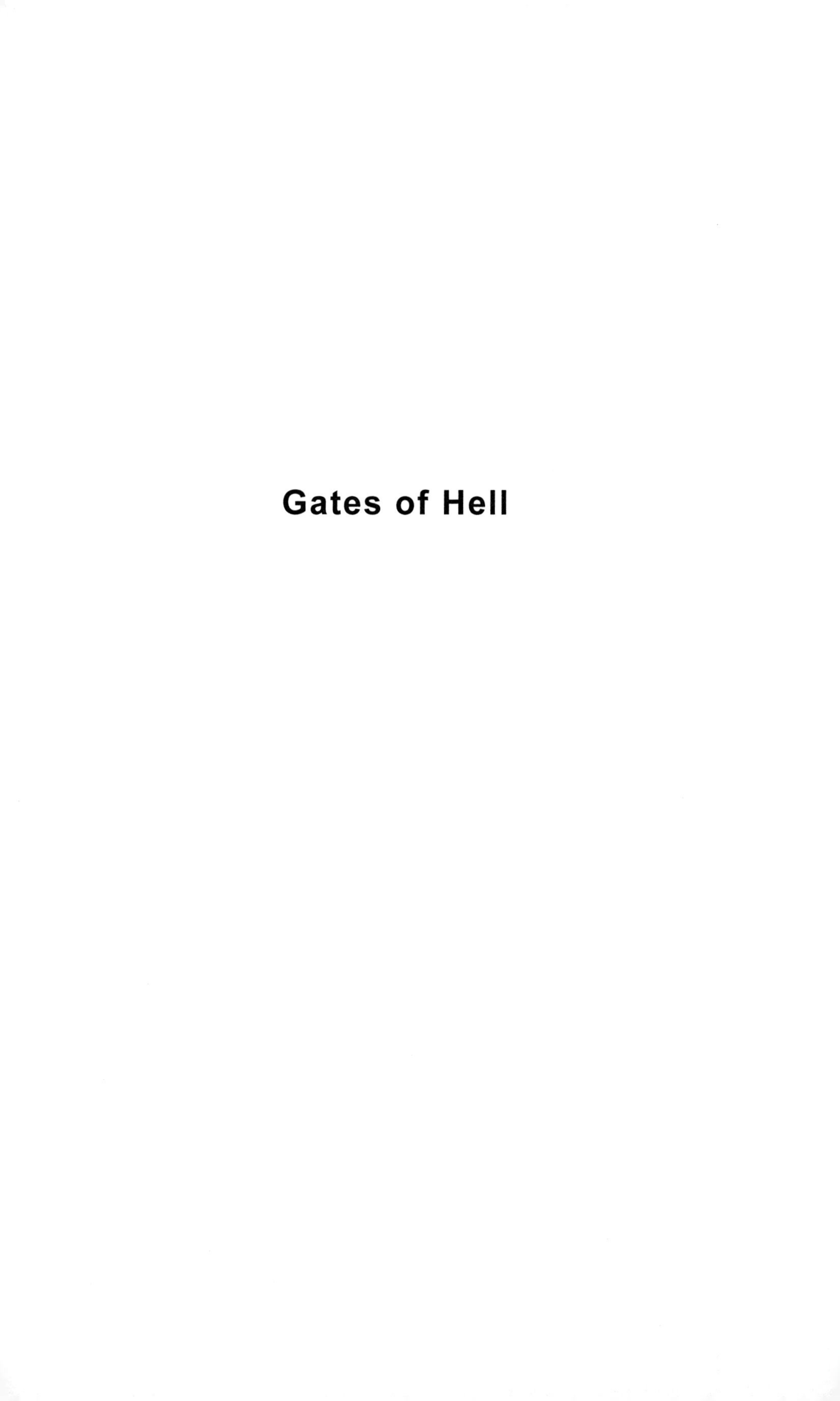

Gates of Hell

Confusion

Let me see. I need the number 9B bus. Let me check to see if it stops here. Being unfamiliar with this place I have got to make sure. I sure hope it runs. It is better. I suppose that is what I get for oversleeping on my way home. Good! It should be here in fifteen minutes. Not even a bench. Oh, there was one but it was beat up and destroyed from what I can tell. I don't understand. Twenty minutes have gone by and nothing. Let me check that thing again. This time with my glasses. Oh no! Well, now I've done it. I am looking at the wrong schedule. Not for an hour. Wonderful! Not a living soul and not even a two-bit coffee shop. Great! It's starting to rain. Not even an umbrella! What a mess! Now I'm going to get soaked. Trying to get rid of this nagging pneumonia and all this now. Achoo! Cough. Cough. Ugh! Where are my cough drops? Empty. Argh! I guess I better start walking back. What a bad scene for a nice girl like me to be in. Completely desolate and spooky. Sounds like my ex. Oh well, here we go. Hey, a cab. Great! He's stopping. Need a ride, miss? Yes, thank you. Where to? The address is 467 3rd. Miss, I think I am going to take a very short nap because the trip shouldn't be too long. You can say that again. What was that? Oh, nothing. Just a little humor. I am sorry. No problem. Here we go! Hey! There is somebody else lost just like me. Hey, cabbie, do your good deed and go get that guy. Besides, he looks kinda cute. A little grayish but it will do. No, ma'am. He does not look like he is lost. I can assure he is not lost. Besides, this guy looks a little dangerous to me. How so? A gun disguised as a broken umbrella. If you don't collect him, you will lose your fare when I jump out. I don't think your boss would appreciate that. Uh, I think you're right. Hey fella! Come on in. My name is Lucy. It looks like we both are lost or stuck or whatever. That's a fair statement my dear Lucy. And your name good looking? It's not important. Okay Mr. Not Important. Where to bud? Haven't we met before cabbie or should I say Elmo? How did you know my name? It says it on your id card. Oh! Yeah. Also I think I know your boss or at least am aware of him. He doesn't show his face too often and then only those who he wishes.

Right, Elmo? And your cab? Why is it such a bright red, like a flame red? Right, Elmo? I don't know who or what you are talking about. This is what they give me. Hey brother, I am just trying to make a living and...My friend Elmo, you choose your words incorrectly. You mean make a...That's enough bud. You gotta get out but the girl stays. What is going on, Mr. Not! You see my dear Lucy, you are genuinely lost or were. You missed your stop because your life was a total confusion. A life of complete and utter chaos. You selected the easy way out. This boyfriend. That boyfriend. The one-night stand at the bar two weeks ago and so on and so forth. An endless chain of events that were meaningless culminating in you being here tonight. However, something was detected, like a pulse but only stronger and deeper. A hint or should I say a whiff of an atom that is so ingrained in your makeup that it is only known to you and a select chosen. Yes, you are lost but you are now found. You have seen the light in the window and it beckons you. Like a crying baby, you needed attention and it was heard. Come, Lucy. Come with me. It is dry and the buses run all night. Here it is. Elmo, you must toil in the mire that you have created for yourself. You have no light, only a dim bulb that may go out at any second. Your penance is not complete. For eternity you will drive around in circles and never run out of gas. Lucy, it is time. Yes, Mr. Not Important, it is time.

Etc. – Part 1 (A Trilogy)

Louise? Oh Louise? Yes, dear? I can't seem to find my glasses. I just had them no more than five minutes ago. These blasted things. I can never find them when I am looking for them! Perhaps if you start not looking for them you'll know where they'll be at all the time. I don't appreciate your sarcasm. And I don't appreciate always telling you they are on your head! We're even. Okay? At least for the next five minutes, Ned. Now. Fine. The coffee, Louise. Don't you remember you told me to make you a strong cup of tulip-tree herbal tea? Why would I tell you that? Tulips don't grow on trees. Why would I tell you nonsense like that since the illogical world is foreign to me? Beats the devil out of me but that's what you wanted and that's what you got. Well whatever it is, I don't want it so drink it yourself. I am not up with herbal teas and I am not going to drink it. Here, you drink it or throw the stuff down the drain. I am not. It took me half way across this god-forsaken place to find this stuff and I am not wasting it. All right, just leave it. The tulip-tree people can have it. Fine. You still want your coffee? No. Not now. Forget it. Louise, if I need you, I'll call you. Suit yourself. Let's see here. My notes. My notes. Lou...Oh never mind. I will look for them myself. I don't need to get yelled at anymore for today and lose my concentration. Here they are. Hmm. Hmm. Ah. Hmm. Yes. Yes. That's right. Okay. Okay. But something is missing. The equational theory is missing an element or two, But I can't be sure. That Louise! I would have figured it out or at least been very close. I say that every day with her around. Maybe I should get rid of her. Maybe not. Who else would help me get organized? I could always find another assistant. This whole situation depends on my being coherent, logical, and stable. That's what I'll do. Call the agency and get another sci-student to help me out. After all, they are a dime a dozen. Besides, they'll do anything to get out of classes and moribund lecturers. And I think her usefulness is worn out. It seems like it's been forever with Louise around. Well, I must do what has to be done. Louise, can you come in here, please. Yes. Oh, I thought you might still like your coffee. Why,

Louise, that is awfully considerate of you. No problem. None whatsoever. I always say it takes a good cup of Joe to get one started, especially a person of your stature. Now, what did you want to see me about? Louise, we have been together for many years and it makes this all the more difficult for me. Yes, Ned? Of course, I will give you all the most highest recommendations and a letter from the faculty stating your incredible dedication to the cause of science and its advancement. What are you trying to tell me? But first, have a cup of that coffee. It is a special brew that has been specially imported with a secret ingredient known only to the farmers from which it is cultivated. Yes. Hmm. Hmm. Wow. This is great. Now, back to what I was saying. Ned, before you continue, I feel you are losing grip with this project and yourself in general. For instance, that tulip-tree drink that you said you wanted. I never asked for it. OH YOU DID! NO, I DIDN'T! This will get us nowhere. Louise, as of this moment, you are released from this project and return to where ever or whatever you came from. It is you, Ned, who will be released from this project. I don't understand. I don't under…I don't…I…Well Ned, you did.

Etc. – Part 2 (A Trilogy)

My dear Louise, I seem to have misplaced my spectacles. Can you help me find them? Why of course, Professor. You left them in the bathroom next to your shaving kit. They had shaving cream all over them, so I cleaned them up. Thank you so much, Louise. I am not sure what I would do without you, Professor, I am sure you would be just fine. I am simply a helper whose job is to, as they say, help you. You are too funny, my good girl. In case you didn't know, the official hand holder and resident comedian. Oh stop it, Louise! I am laughing and crying at the same time! We'll never get any work done. You are right, Professor. Enough being jocular. That's right. Now, to more important business. I would like to see my notes from the third. Why the third, Professor? Something we did yesterday didn't seem quite right. Such as? When we did the experiment number Four-B. The end didn't come out as I thought it should. It was a little off and I need to make a correction so as to prove it right. Okay, Professor. Here we are. Thank you, Louise. Now, let's see. Hmm. Hmm. That is not making sense. What is, Professor? Everything matches. The numbers. The ingredients. The everything. Do you remember what we did to get the correct result? No, I didn't Professor. Wait a minute! You took off that day. You said you had an important appointment to keep. You must be mistaken, Professor. I was here all day. What I actually said was that I had an important appointment but I canceled it because I knew you were on route to a very key step in your experiments. Louise, I feel quite confident that you were not here. They sent me over an intern to help with my notes. I remember clearly. Her name was Joyce Wilson. She is a second-year student. She stayed past six because she had trouble reading my bad script. Her name should be listed as the transcriber. Here we go. It says…What does it say, Professor? It has your name, Louise. Now, Professor…Now what Louise? Something is not right here. You are correct, Professor. The only thing not right is you. How dare you say that to me! No! How dare you say that to me. It seems that your work has been quite shoddy, lately. Missing this. Forgetting that. An important project in the annals of mankind. There is next to no room for error. Louise...Don't Louise me, Professor! From what I can see, there is no room for you, Professor!

Etc. – Part 3 (A Trilogy)

Good evening, Louise. Good evening, Professor Michaels. I apologize for the lateness of our study but I was tied up in meetings regarding funding and the like. Not a problem professor. I have always been a night person myself but standards and proper research etiquette require that I work during the day. How about you, Louise? Myself, Professor Michaels, any time is my time in the name of science and discovery. Very good thinking! I suppose that is why you make such an excellent and trustworthy assistant. However, Louise, I sense you do your best work late in the day and overnight. I appreciate your praise and question your supposition on my work habits. It was not meant to be an insult or a discredit to your work but a mere observation on my part in that I have been around a long time and generally, a good judge of character. So Louise, if you take it the wrong way, I do apologize. Accepted, Professor Michaels. Accepted. Now back to our work. May I have yesterday's notes and another cup of your world-famous coffee? Here are your notes and the coffee. I thought that you might like a cup sensing the hour. Absolutely. Now, drink up, professor and let's get started. Hmm. This coffee is very good! What do you call this concoction? "The Last Drop" is its name. Very intriguing. Very intriguing indeed. Why the name? You'll find out very shortly, professor. It seems we have been wasting time on false premises and theories. Louise, and pray tell what are they? I am not going to tell you because it is a waste of time since your life is ticking down. Louise, it is you whose time is ticking down. What do you mean, professor? I would like to have you meet my other assistant who has been with me for the longest time, Gabe. Otherwise, known as Gabriel. Gabriel, hand me my walking stick. Thank you. You see, Louise, we have been following you for the longest time. I cannot believe you do not recognize me. How is your neck and back? Has it straightened its curve or is it permanent? Your belly, is it well-worn or do you not care? Yes Louise, we know who you are. We are very old friends. You idol worshiper! You lovers of the clean and proper disgust me. I have made it my role in my time to make everybody believe that you are no good and whose apex is a false god! My brethren who I have drawn to me know the truth! Pigs! All of you pigs! You're a lover of others and all is supreme folly destined to fall under my control! My control! Not yours but mine! I will never give up! As long as there is one entity with doubts of your crass existence I shall win. And win. And win! No, Louise. You will never win. You will only exist at the behest of the One who rules all. Your false accusations are for the weak and then, still, subservient for we will win in the long run. Your destiny is tied up to ours. Your foul stench and looks will be your downfall. Now, the cane is another weapon for use against your nonsense. You should remember it well. It perforated your foul flesh and sealed you to the ground. It is a weapon against you that will be used time and time and time again. As a matter of fact, till the end of all. See! You have reverted back already! Under my foot and spear behind your neck! You are commanded to obey and leave this place infected by your worms and slime! Gabriel, let us go for our work is done again. Michael, I fear it will never end. Yes it will. We were there when assurance was given that it will. As one person may be left, it is ours to be there. And there. And there. And over there.

Flesh

Hand me a scalpel, nurse. Thank you. That looks nice, I should be an artist or butcher or something. I'll take a side of beef, doctor. You are too much, Maggie! Too much! I guess that is why we get along together so well. Okay, yeah sure. Get some absorbent. A couple of gallons have leaked out. Let's scoop it up and pour it back in. Alright, that's done. Let's take a look in here. That looks pretty bad. Just about all this stuff gotta' go. From there to there and a bit over there. What a mess! Maggie what did you do after you left here after a 20-hour stretch? Believe it or not, I stayed up because I was so backlogged on my bills. Any sleep? About an hour. That was just before I came back here. Yuck! Let us see. I need a number 26. Here, doctor. Hmm. Hmm. I sure could use a little liquid wrench. Give me a uh, uh, a number 37 right. There we go. Much better. There goes that pesky blood, again. Sop that up, nurse. Yuck! Certainly a mess. Huh, doctor? What are you going to do? Back to the meat counter. Some cat gut. Put your finger there. Okay. It isn't pretty but it works. Wish I could use some gum to hold everything together or to plug a hole. Next case. Right there under that very bleak looking piece of flesh. It is a bleaker looking thing than its neighbor. You ain't kidding, doc. You know what? What? Friends should never leave friends or a great neighborhood. So what'll we do is take the entire neighborhood and its residents and find a nice, quiet spot for them in the trash burner. But doctor, should everybody be punished? Good point, nurse, but the good goes with the bad. From what I see, there wasn't much good going on in there, anyway. Okay. Bucket. And there we go! Almost done. Now what? What is this? All that mess. Where, doctor? There! Can't you see it? See what? That! That what! I must be tired. I swear there were globs of goo just oozing from behind that tissue. Come to think of it, doctor, yes. Now I see it! I was concerned, nurse, on your lack of observation. Um, you know what, you are right! Let's sew this guy up and let him enjoy his life that he's got left. A morphine drip for our patient. When he wakes up. We'll tell him the news. You mean, YOU will tell him the news.

Okay, you win. Hello, Mr. Kravitz? This is your doctor speaking. Yes. Ooh. Everything is hurting. Why am I not going to get better? Unfortunately not. You see, Mr. Kravitz, you have not paid your bill. I pay all of my bills and you will get paid too. In this case, someone else. Mr. Kravitz I represent a client who demands full payment, no installment plan, and does not accept credit. I do not know who you mean! As a bill collector yourself, you can understand my predicament. You see I am a doctor today. Tomorrow, I could be a duck hunter. The next, a drunk driver. And so on and so on. I deliberately botched your surgery so would have no choice but to accept my client's claim. You see Mr. Kravitz, you have but moments to live. You will have brutal pain. Your eyes will roll back. If you could, you would double over and fall to the floor. However, not today. No dramatics since we are so short on time and I must get paid. Goodbye, Mr. Kravitz and enjoy your trip to the salt mines.

Gameshow

Ladies and gentlemen – and I use that term loosely! – welcome to our Sunday Night Edition of "Who are You?" As you already know, during the week we select a member of the studio audience and bring him down to the, pardon the expression, the hot seat! Here the panelists will try to figure the reason for the importance of this person or if the person is not important at all, the punishment for trifling their valuable time when they could have fun like the good ole Romans did. At the last moment, however, one of the most important personages – again I mean important, well known, most influential, and a helluva pinochle player, is with us here tonight. And as an added bonus, the panelist who guesses correctly will win an all-expense paid, tax free and no passport needed – ooh boy I am getting chills up and down my spine – for themselves and their closest 300 friends – a trip to the paradise that our great guest tonight calls home. But first, let me introduce the esteemed and I might say, highly charged and motivated panelists. The gentleman to left is himself a well-known and great friend of the ladies, the effervescent Joe Phland. Joe, what have you been – pardon the expression – up to? The usual stuff Harry, you know, this and that, but with mostly that and well whoever is around, if you get my drift. Joe, it stinks to high, well you know but we won't go there. Okay Joooooooooe! To Joe's left is the bubbly and oh so curvy Peaches, just Peaches. Hey Peach, how did you get that name? Well how do you think I did? Are you blind? It was better than being called Mel – oh never mind Har. You' re such a card! If I may say, the Ace of Spades! Alright already! Flattery will get you everywhere, right Joe? Harry, my stinky friend, only to the Pad of Joe! Ugh! Well be that as it may, the last but not least a fine and improper gentleman of the British aristocracy, who spends most of his time trampling on grapes and squeezing some, Lord Byron of Oestville. Welcome to our humblest and breakaway shores. Well thank you my dear Harry. Always a pleasure to see how the colonists are doing, their Puritanical and nauseously nauseous selves. You are too kind M' Lord. Now shut your blimey coated gob Byron and sit there like a good snob! You win young Harold! You win. Okay with the panelists and now the crux of the matter – oops – I meant the fire of the night. Now, here is our guest and gruntiness himself sitting behind the darkened shades of secrecy and twilight and who has allowed me to give one clue. That clue is – drum-rolls please! It is someone who has touched everyone's life. Let's start with our friend from across the sea Lord Oestville. Thank you Harry. Good evening Mr. Guest. Are you bigger than a breadbasket? Did I hear you say sometimes? You did. Okay. Quite interesting. It looks like your shadow is morphing into something else. Are you a quick-change artist or magician? Yes, that too. Hmm. I pass. Okay! Ladies next – Peaches? Thanks a load Har. My gosh you must be good lookin'. I can now see a very distinguished nose and a wide brim hat – I think. Are you a relative of Casanova? Oh you are Casanova or you are a Casanova? You are, huh. I give up. Where is that martini you promised me, Harry. Oh screw it. Well, we now come to the genuiuass of the group, Mr. Encyclopedia and purveyor of all things sordid, Joe. Go ahead Joe you get the last stab at our guest. Before I start asking questions Harry, something is very odd here. I keep looking at our guest and he seems to change appearance or size or shape or something. I am sober so I can't be seeing things. And even when I am loaded, I can still tell things. Wait...OH NOOOOOO! NOOOOOOOOOOooooooo! MY JOE! MY JOE! MY JOE! COME TO ME! COME TO ME! COME TO ME ALL OF YOU! COME TO ME! BUT NOT YET. YOUR TIME IS NOT NIGH! I AM PATIENT FOR I TOO HAVE ETERNAL AGES! I CHALLENGE ALL THAT IS ABHORRENT TO ME! YOU AND YOUR SACRAMENTS AND YOUR HOCUS POCUS AND HOLIER THAN THOUS AND YOUR TAMBOURINES AND THE UNLEAVEN BREAD. I WAIT AND I LURK AND I STEAL YOUR SOUL IN THE NIGHT, THE BACK ALLEY, THE PULPIT, THE CRADLE, AND FINALLY THE GRAVE. COME JOE WITH ME THE PROMISE YOU MADE. I QUENCHED YOUR THIRST! YOU TOO WILL NEVER BE DRY! HA HA HA HA HAAAAAA! Peaches and Oestville you guys will be back for round two of this get together. The guest for the next and final round has allowed himself to give you folks a hint of his identity. He was once almost the world leader; his favorite drink was schnapps and could paint a room – two coats in one afternoon. But first, a word from our sponsor Ole' Smokey – the product that is good for a hotfoot.

Gates of Hell

There was a man backslapping another, though he wasn't known for this. Normally, he was dour and sullen. Seeming as though the world – or so he thought – was against him, he maintained a conservative and civil appearance to the throngs and even to those around him. This day, he felt, was a culmination of a lifetime of rejection and hate that would be turned into a resurrection avenging this culture. In reality, the embers began to stir and a wind blew foul.

There was another man. This time, a man confident and self-assured. A man who could lead a mega-mega company and not think twice about the decisions made. A self-made man? Not in the literal sense but in a surreal kind of way. A CEO of a major company? Yes! There were no shareholders but people in search of a service. We see him on a podium. Hands outstretched on the corners as though he was giving a dissertation on the works of Plato or the latest financial report. None of these was ever closest to the truth. The environs were pitch black with no visible lights but all was seen clearly. In the far-off distance, one could see a tall steel structure. It appeared to be burning but giving off no light to the surroundings – as though a shroud was engulfing its luminosity. Throngs of beings – all faceless and nondescript – occupied the view of this man. Other than this man, the only thing clear was a flag. Drooping but held high, it was a green with yellow or gold markings. The meaning was only known to this man and whoever he wished to be part of his council. And there he stood…

The backslapping man no longer exists. He is in front of a small group of people in a formal setting. They are all crying and the dour man does his best to control his own feelings. His thoughts and words go back and forth, this way and that, confusion and serenity. All are interlaced with hate and anger and vengeance. All this despite his pleas for rationality. He then leaves with his wife and departs as he came – waving and full of revenge.

Locker Room

It was sunny and clear. In the bay, one could see a large ocean-going vessel maneuvering toward the open sea. It was constructed with an unending amount of passenger compartments and space for nothing else. In this case, however, no reservations were required. There were no flags. No markings. Nothing to identify the owner or origins of this beast. A simple ocean-going vessel painted the standard white and red.

Once in a Lifetime

"I must do this before I die!" shouted the medieval cleric in red robes. He jumps two or three stories from an inside balcony and lands face down spread eagle. A moment or two later, a mysterious, nebulous figure arises and starts to walk away.

Pasta

Good afternoon, Miss Thomas. Good afternoon, Mr. Taft. How may I help you today? I am looking for something with good marbling, but not too much. Sounds to me, Miss Thomas, like you would like a statue, probably of David. You are too funny, Mr. Taft. Who's being funny? I thought you were, Miss Thomas. You know, you might be just right. Statues are nice, but the real thing would be fantastic. Miss Thomas, we only sell the real thing. Wow! I am sure it would be or should I say, he would be priceless. I'll put it on your tab. But I don't have one. Now you do, Miss Thomas. You are more than generous with your goods. I am sure you will like the goods! Just step over where it says, "Pickup". Thank you, Mr. Taft. Thank you, Miss Thomas. Next! Hello, Mr. Fellows. Hello, Mr. Taft. I am not sure what or how to describe it. Just tell me and I will figure something out. Okay, deal. Looking for about an order of one-hundred pounds. That could be expensive, Mr. Taft. Worry about that later. Now just tell me and I will help you as much as I can. Sure. Lean but not too lean. A little fat is okay. Medium rare will work. And I can't think of anything else. Gottcha! The bill – I am not sure I can pay it off. Don't worry, Mr. Fellows. We are all friends here. I'll set up an account for you. Well, thank you Mr. Taft. No, thank you. It's my pleasure to serve you. Just go over to the place where it says, "Pickup". Okay. Bye. Next! Oh! Nobody left. That is strange. Oh, Bobby? Yes, pop. I need you to make the rounds again. Where to this time? Let me check the list. Hmm. This one. Let me see, pop. I was just there a week ago. I know, but those folks are rife for the picking. Okay. On my way. Cheryl? Yes, dad? Time to make another trip. I am a little tired. Can't I take a break? Alright. Have a snack and a lie down but be out by two. Sure, pops. Let me see. Hmm. Hmm! Oh, hello little Timmy. What can I do for you? A friend? Yes, a friend? You are very popular, why would you need a friend. I need a friend who thinks I am great. Who thinks I can do anything and is always there when I need him. What makes you think I can get you a friend? After all, this is a butcher shop. Why don't you go over to City Park. There are a lot of kids over there. Both boys and girls play there. I know this is a butcher shop but you seem always to have the right answers to everything. You are very helpful and you are spoken of highly. Well, thank you Timmy. I think I have just what you need. Just go over where it says “Pickup” and walk right in. Thank you, Mr. Taft. Thank you, Jimmy! Nobody here. Great! A chance to take a break. What a day! Nonstop from when we opened to now. Whew! Business is good. Numbers are up. Oh, two customers. I like that. Gentlemen! We are here from the health department and would like to inspect your establishment. To begin with, we need to see your certificates. I…I…We thought so. We have your certificates. You have violated the terms beyond repairable means. Example, three weeks ago, you persuaded someone that you didn’t think they needed to shop here. We let that go. However, it happened again and again and again. Worst of all, on Sundays. Mr. Taft, we are concerned that you are helping the competition. They don’t need any help. We are still ahead and it will remain that way. You have become soft and forgiving. Kinder and gentler. Guilty and guiltier of yourself and less harsh of others. Our tradition is of service – ours. I am sorry to say Mr. Taft, you can longer be in ours. Now, it is your turn at the “Pickup” window.

Pay Your Fare

There were two men dressed in black.
There was an old woman.
They were all in a subway car.
One said to the woman: You won't be scared if we empty the bullets?
The woman sat there stony faced.
Unmoving – like a cutout figure.
Or even dead.
As the train left, one man patted the side of the subway car.

Purity

It was white. Completely. There were three people – two men and one woman. Even what they were wearing was white – was it a spacesuit or was it for cold weather? That is not important. But what is important is that the scraggly looking man shouted, “When I drop this leaf, someone must die!” Then, a scream erupted. All that were left were two – a man with only a right eye and a nondescript looking woman?

Ragamuffin

The temporal lobe is damaged doctor. Yes it is. Quite clear. Quite clear. It appears to be the usual these days. Very much of a rash or properly spoken, epidemic. Any ideas, doctor? The usual: greenhouse effects, lead in the water, sodas with globs of sugar and so on and so forth. So many young people with the same affliction and all at the same time. We poke and prod, have them take a big green pill at night and tell us how they are in the morning. And all for naught! My my! Anything else, doctor? No thank you. I'll try some new things, like getting one plus one to equal Pi. That would be some scientific breakthrough! Or perhaps, a miracle, doctor? I am too far from the door to walk but close enough to be carried. Good night, doctor. Good night to you.

Slaves

The venue was an enormous structure. Bigger than anything ever built or conceived by man. In this case, that is not the case nor is it in the realm of touch. Countless. Nameless. Faceless. That is the intent. All are men. All are young. All wearing scarlet dress coats. All clean cut. Not facing inward to the arena but outward to the walls. There are ushers. They are wearing green dress coats. Not that anyone one is trying to leave but decorum is important to the organizer. The scene is set.

The Man with a Plan (?)

The scene is – and like all else under the sun (does it still exist?) – is bleak and dreary. The man driving the train is looking for an appropriate (is there a right one?) destination (the end of the line?) There is no certainty but chooses one to his liking (there is only one who knows and he is not saying.)

Worms

Dillingham, come here. Yes, M' Lord Abbish? Fetch my top coat and hat, along with my cane. Which one, sir? Oh, yes, the brass one. Yes sir. Once you do that, call the carriage man for I am going hunting. Yes, right away sir. Now where is my case? Dillingham, sorry to bother you ole' chap but have you seen my case? If you recall sir, I believe it to be in the wall safe. Oh yes. Thank you. Let me see, to the right, left, to the right again and there we are. A fresh supply and we are off. M' Lord, the carriage awaits. See you in the morning, Dillingham. Godspeed to you M' Lord. Masters, I am ready. Here is where we must go. Yes, M' Lord. A little cup of juice and I will be ready. Very refreshing. Very refreshing indeed. Here is the location you requested, sir. Thank you, Masters. You may leave. And remember, pick me up in exactly four hours and not a word to anyone. Yes, M' Lord. Let me see. Hmm. Hmm. Just what I thought I would find. But this is much more than usual. However, I will be ready for just such a situation. La la la de la la. Can't remember the rest but enjoyed the song much more in my earlier days. What's this? Well hello there. Can you tell me the way to Effingham? My carriage was robbed and my carriage man was killed back on the Old School Road. Any assistance would be greatly appreciated my good friend. Can you not speak? I gather that is a no or you have a very bad cold. You can hear? Argh. That seems to be a yes. Well then if you cannot help me, at least do not hinder me on my way back to civilization. Step aside then and let me pass. I said please move so that I can be on my way before the rain sets in. Argh. Argh. Then, is it your master I seek or is he seeking me? Argh. Argh. Argh. I see you have some friends. I guess I will go with you. Chaps, not so fast for I am almost elderly and slow to start. Not much better but a little for I am in no position to argue. Welcome to my abode my Lord Abbish! I see you keep many friends and your daily bathing habit is nil. Abbish, you constantly amuse me. I didn't know this was a parlor show. Mind yourself, Abbish! So, what is it you want from me? A truce or at least no more than a break of you versus me. For how long? About thirty years will suffice. Thirty years? Yes. I figure you will be in a bad way at St. Paul's graveyard. Intriguing! And what makes you think I am going somewhere since we have been dueling all these ages? I can be optimistic about such things for within me, are the molecules of longevity. You are just a bag of bones and soiled meat. I don't think so my mortal enemy. Are you going to have something to do with it? I might or I might not. You must use what is called a brain that is used for a hat rack. I like the brain and the hat exactly where they are. You amuse me with your gallows humor. You see! Even I can be funny and personable. It's the personable part that doesn't work for you. Your humor does not escape you even in the final hour Abbish. My Lord Evil ever the optimist. My Lord Nauseam, the soon to be the former. Enough banter! Let us proceed…Uncle, what happened next? Well, let us say I am here telling you this story and that is all you need to know. Perhaps when you are older you will understand without me giving the ending. I hope so, Uncle. No, William, you will. Now, time for bed for the hour is late. I promised your mum you would be in bed by nine so that we may get up early and go fishing in Duke's Pond. Yes, Uncle. Dillingham? Yes, M' Lord? See that the young William is comfortable in his room and tucked in. Yes, M' Lord. I guess it is that time for me too, Thank you, Dillingham. Shall I prepare your evening? Yes, as usual. You are a great help to me in my pursuits and I fear I never will be adequately thankful enough. You are too kind my Lord in your words. If I may speak? You may always speak freely for you have earned the right to. You see, M' Lord, my family has been in this "business" since the earth was made whole. We have been at your side or others who represent your side to assist in this well-worn path. Not the leader nor gun bearer but the supplier of strength and fortitude for the times that these traits must be called upon. My ancient lineage knows no other service and prefers the shadows to the noon day sun. And with that, M'lord, may I turn you in for the evening that is also part of my duties? Dillingham, you spoke well and clear and your point was well taken. Your heritage is noble and is second to none. You and your fore bearers are as an integral part in this scheme as anyone else. You shall be with me when I drink my water and eat my bread and bleed my blood. And if not me, someone like me will be with someone like you. M' Lord Abbish, thank you. No, Dillingham, thank you. I fear another sortie is on tap for tomorrow for the Highlands and that is a longer trip for we must get an early start. Good evening, Dillingham. Good evening M' Lord.

Red Glare

It was night time. The central business district was busy as ever – but not in the usual way. Black and white triangular flying machines infested the air crashing and pounding into anything that stood in the way. Above all this, standing untouched, was a well-lit room on top of the tallest building with two men scurrying about. A man on the ground was heard to say he used to work there but not anymore. To the men in the room it seemed as if nothing was happening. Perhaps just another day at the office.

Historical Fiction

Authority

General, sir, the troops are waiting for the next command. I know, son. I know. It is a heavy burden I and I alone bear. I understand, sir. No disrespect, son, but you don't and you can't. Sorry, General. Accepted, corporal. Now, bring me the charts that are marked K-2. Yes, General. Here they are, sir. Thank you, son. Yes, General. Anything else? Hmm. Hmm. A swag of coffee, if there is any left. Some left, sir. Thank you. You may go now. These maps. These sketches. All unreliable. All full of non-sensible gibberish. These written reports are as contradictory as the days of the year. How can I carry out my duties if all this information is wrong? Even if it has a fifty percent correct rate, that is no good. There is still that other fifty percent which can cause turmoil and utter disaster. My dear! I wish I was home. But, that is not even a welcome place. I suspect, however, anyplace would be better than this hell. We must go on! A true cause of great magnitude and importance is at stake here. We cannot fail. We must press on! The revolution of a lifetime that will free men's souls. An epic battle of good versus evil. The cause for the defeat of tyranny is mighty. The right of self-determination was born generations ago. A new brother will be conceived, free of sin and pollution. The parents will nurture and guide. Correct where needed and observant when required. But this is all useless if I don't have the right information. Corporal! Yes, general? Any report back from our scouts? No, sir. Any messages from anybody? None, sir. Any idea if the enemy is reinforcing himself? Again, no, sir. I might as well have a blindfold on each one of our soldiers. That will be all, corporal. Yes sir. Dear God, please that I do your will. I will either be sending you the heathen, who will most likely be rotting in hell or my beloved sons, who will sit at your right hand. Amen. Sound the alert! George, you are the only one left who has the resolve and the knowledge to present a great gift to our mother. I will certainly try, General. Godspeed! Oh my dear Lord! What is happening? My own shame is building! The men! The men! They are falling like matchsticks! I fear the reality is setting like a haze over a pall. Many dead. Many are not going home to be a father! What children will not be born! What parents to grieve! It is all my fault! No one else. Mine and mine alone! I shall never be free even after I have returned to Mother Earth! George! George! Regroup and attack. General, I have no troops left. This horrible place! This place of death! Oh my sons! I would gladly give myself for all these brave children! This soil is evil! This air is poisoned! Let us go home. Let us leave this accursed place of Yankee vomit! Let us leave this place of Pennsylvania!

Baggit!

What troubles you woman? It is you my husband. We're not going to start that again. Start what my witch? I shall ignore your brutality and ugliness and tell you. The way you don't like my unrefinement? Or is it the friends I keep – especially my woman friends? Obviously that is part of it but not wholly. Your men friends? You mean my loyal dogs? NO! The friend or who you at least thought was your friend whose ego and self-righteousness got in the way. At least you wouldn't try to sleep with him or are you? Woman, mind your tongue! I am still boss around here and would more than happy to have your putrid little self-dangling off a battlement. Now silence and go away. I must contemplate worldly things which would cause that thing above your neck to explode like a melon! Go! Send in our ecclesiastical friend. You sent for me? Yes I did. All these things that he is doing – can't you tell him to stop? Unfortunately not. Those are to say, in the contract, not just for him, but all of us. Don't lecture on these things! I am well aware of my doctrines and stories. I mean those other things. You mean about the public discourse on morals and mores of…Enough! The answer is still no. Within the purview of his office which YOU forced us to accept and crown. Stand clear of those words or I shall shackle you to the horse trow and place a brute sow in your stead. Sorry for the blunted remarks. I shall be more delicate but no less truthful. Get out and collect your alms or I shall stab you with a fork. Yes. But…But nothing! Where is our problem child? Look at that! They pass each other with barely a nod. I love a good fight so as long as I win. Yes, come in. You don't bow anymore? It is not you who I serve. And I will not kiss your ring. So there! Have we put away your child things many a time ago? You act as though you deserve praise from me…From me? I put up nonsense and darkness from my family only because of the lineage required. From you, I will not tolerate such tripe and take that ego of yours and pluck it out with a fork or spoon or whatever this thing is called. It is called a spoon and is used to take liquids form a bowl or cup and bring it to your mouth and…I cannot stay angry with you. We have been friends way to long for a title to get between us, Not mine, but yours. But you made that decision for me and I pleaded on my fathers' soul not carry it on my shoulder. It was no Emmaus but it sufficed. I now carry the burden lightly but take its meaning heavily. I find it refreshing to breathe the air of humbleness and purity amongst the common folk. Are you saying I stink? Only if you are not use to the smell. I am not sure what that means but I will let it go because of my magnificence. Anyway mostly because of our long and esteemed past. Remember the times we went on trips to countryside and we had great times integrating with the folk? In your case, the female folk. Absolutely! I needed to make sure our lady stock was up to producing a fine and healthy population needed to sustain our way of life. Okay. But it is a different cloak I wear now. It is one of a longer tradition and thicker wool. It has tears and lice which represent the fabric of society and bruises of people. These things are inflicted upon me in the style you have given me but I wear it well and gladly in the role. I often think in my life's choices this should have been the first. However, in your wisdom you have instituted that new role and for you that comes easily and that is why you are where you are and I am where I am. You know, that is why I will always like you – you are almost as smart as I am. I wish we could be on the same team again. But we are! We are all human! That is a great team! We all want to cross the finish line first. And we will! Each one of us starts the race differently so we will always win. This, no matter who we think is in front or who is on our heels! I love your logic but it is flawed. You have the free will to just act the part and carry on with our friendship but you choose not to. But…But nothing! Go away before I do something rash like see my family and listen to their advice. Remember my Lord Henry: teamwork. Remember your Eminence Thomas: friendship.

Changeling

Good period of time to you sir. And to your sir. I have called you for a special and most unusual task. Thank you for your consideration, sir. Yes. Very yes, sir. Now that we have the perfunctory greetings completed, I wish to state the meaning of the purpose of our discussion. Yes, I am listening. You were selected for this task in that not only one the senior members here, you are the most positively reviewed being on the staff and with the highest success rate. I believe 97.2%. Is that correct, sir? I do my errands to the best of my abilities and with that rate at not 100%, I feel I have failed in my purpose. Your modesty is gratifying and does not suit you. You are destined for higher callings. Thank you, sir for your confidence and hope that the task you will assign will be as successful as the 97.2% from the past. I am strongly positively suited for your goal will be attainable and if the past is a prologue, we must deny it in the present. Well taken, sir. Well taken. I shall do my best and nothing less. Thank you for those words. Now, what your goal will be will be none of your concern. What we are seeking is the final result. Your main objective will be transmitted to you the usual way and all packages – a main one and should I say spares – will be released once your knowledge is complete. If you are successful, the age of glory will come upon all those who yearn it and those who not, will gnash their teeth until their gums are bloodied and tongue is ruptured. Sir, a most important task you have assigned me. I am still not certain I am the one to carry out this supreme. Nay, speak no more, sir. You have been selected to perform this thing. Your modesty stands in the way of clear thinking. Set aside this virtue of yours and educate those who need to be instructed. Those who need to be cleansed. Those who need it. Sir, I will go and do this but please do not berate me or scorn me if I should fail. If you do fail, the mission will continue on for the eras to come and those like you will go forth and pray for success. Go now. Go now and do not dwell on your 97.2%. But please dwell on pure thought and pure light. Sir, I go now with your blessing. The blessings of multitudes are yours however which way the boat drifts. Be gone, sir. Be gone! I am here. This place. This time. This street. People of non-descriptive character going about their normal chores. Nothing out of the ordinary. Nothing to derive for me the purpose of my visit. Not a hint. Not a gleam. Not a minuscule of grain for me to chew on. I must remember that it is not for me to speculate nor prejudge on the discourse of these people or time. So be it. I am here. It must be done. Ah, this is the place. Nothing unordinary about. A simple dwelling. I must mark the time – April 20, 1889. The place – a small village in a large state called Austria. I feel the time is approaching. It must be quick. It must be clean. It must be in the blink of an age. I am ready. I feel 100%. I feel the weight of a million universes on my shoulders. I will carry them on my back and take up the yoke given me. It is time. The door. The name. It reads: Hiedler.

Conversion

Now what do I do? I have never had any problems making decisions in the past. Here I am today with my colleagues. I am not sure they are my friends. They could be trusted once and once again because it suited their needs and inspirations. Today, here in this place, only a few are left. All the others fled. They were only worried about their own hides. They once pledged their very lives to me and the ideals. When push came to shove, they showed their true colors – dark and empty. But, all this mentalizing is not productive to me at this moment. The world is closing in. The sky is red and black. Pandemonium is all around. I cannot see it, but I sense it. My very boots quiver as each second passes. I have seen this before and came out intact. Well, mostly. My mind remains sharp and clear. My body shakes uncontrollably. It is most annoying that I – the majesty of my being – is racked by troublesome atoms. We have the finest doctors in the world and this disease cannot be cured. Most likely they were activated by the anarchists who attempted to curtail our great scheme. They paid the price for heresy and disloyalty. The doctors were part of that conspiracy. I feel that I could be one hundred percent if not for their feigned incompetence and dubious explanations. They were sent somewhere cold to rethink their medical careers. Fortunately, I am here with the only person who always stayed with me through thick and now the thin. She is a wonderful person who loves me for who I really am – lonely and misunderstood. How I wish all the others had half of her constitution! Just a moment, the wall could use another coat of paint. Perhaps a bright color instead a drab gray. Something to think about. There is my girl! She livens this hole with her rainbow of color – her garb and her mind! It pains me that I never really had the courage to ask her to be my wife. I tried to rationalize it by saying that I would be very busy and could not spend time with her on the veranda or enjoy her tea parties. I cannot say that now. The time is 'nigh and short. I commanded her to be my wife. No objections. So it was! And now, it is almost time for the last hurrah. The last of everything. I have my doubts about a higher being but I shall find out soon. I feel that I will be judged harshly and perhaps rightly so. That is why I am scared, not how it will end, but how it will end. I am so sorry. Where is my wife? Dearest, it is time. I know you love me and you have been a good person. I have not. I shall not see you on the other side but will be looking up at you with a tear on my face and prongs in my heel. My epitaph:

The Fuhrer and his wife…

Guilt

Gene, I am not envious of your position. Louis, I struggle every day. My entire being is twisted. I have been through many crises and suffer each one. I am always at a loss. My thoughts are bleak and unforgiving. I grow old quicker than the calendar. This thing will never end in my heart, though it will end physically. Gene, I pray every day that you will do the right thing. I, as well. Sometimes I think that my own prayers will be answered and other times, not. A difference between the two may lie in just the middle – not yes, nor no, but maybe. It is not for us to decide, Gene. I realize that, Louis, but at the very core of our being we always hope for the positive. But at what cost, Gene? I believe at the cost of our soul. We will never know the answer until the end. And by then, who will care? Will it be the gravedigger by the cold expression on our face? Or will it be the last word uttered? Yes, Louis it will be too late. Gene, you are too pessimistic about things. People look up to you for guidance and love. How can I even do that when I can't even do that myself. "Physician, heal thyself" was once uttered or would you prefer "Let the dead bury the dead"? Louis, you constantly amaze me. Perhaps you should be here instead of I. No, Gene, you were put here for a reason and I for another. The power behind the throne? No, just the man who helps his friend hold up his staff. Thank you for your friendship, Louis. Thank you for your love, Gene. Now, back to the task that faces us. You know Louis, I so fear for the safety of our mother. She must never fall and be squeezed around her neck. If she must, Gene, she must. If she is squeezed, she is squeezed. That is what everybody signs up for. She may come out bruised, but bruises heal and will be stronger for it. That is how this thing started – through pain and suffering and much squeezing. But we are here to talk about it, Gene, and it is your responsibility to see her through – perhaps as a healer or even as midwife. But it must be done with all your moral authority and I suspect, with some intrigue. Louis, you are as right as the day is long. My moral authority is very weak, to say the least, but I have been trained by the very best at intrigue. For the good, Gene?

Yes, for the good, Louis. Now, what we originally discussed. How soon can we make arrangements for the first phase? Gene, I know your mind and heart and have already taken steps for its implementation. Louis, there you are again! Yes, Gene, I knew in my heart of hearts that you would carry this through. Morally and ethically it is the right thing to do. No fanfare. No grand oratories. No grand parades. No grand indignations. No beating of the chest. Just simple acts by simple and humble servants of our mother. I often pray for forgiveness that we have not or ever could do enough. It is for this reason, Louis, that I suffer. Gene, as you said before, we will never know to the very end. I believe you are right, Louis. Now, to the more mundane. You have an audience with visiting dignitaries from Asia. I welcome to see you, my brothers. We welcome to see you, Holy Father.

Papa's Little Boy

Mr. Wentz. Mr. Wentz? What do you want? The landlord said you live here and...Go away! You are not needed here! Go away! The landlord said you have a problem and we are here...Go away or I will call the...Willy, come here! Yes, papa? Dinner is almost ready. And what is mama cooking? Your favorite of potatoes and chicken broth. I cannot wait, papa. But first, Willy. Yes, papa? As I have asked your brothers I must ask you. Papa? What would you like to be when you are of age? A soldier. A soldier? Yes, papa. A very important and serious job. But why, Willy? I like the uniform, papa. Remember, the man makes the uniform not the other way around...Please open the door, Mr. Wentz. I have told you once please leave! I am a sick man and I can't be disturbed. But the landlord...Well, Joseph, I am glad to see you here. I am glad to see you also, Willy. And there is the lovely Christine. Not bad for a revolutionary or starving artist, Willy? Even a starving artist, Christine. Aside from the perfunctionaries, is he here? Yes, there he is. Quite engrossing. Along with about a dozen agents from the other side. Can a short man be successful? Napoleon for example. Quite correct. He didn't listen to history and that is why Russia doesn't speak French. Oh, what now? Let's leave. The temperature is rising along with the billy clubs...Get the landlord. This Wentz guy is a lunatic. Please Mr. Wentz, let us in to check the...You over there, that line. You three here. You old hags walk over to spot 12. Come on we haven't got all day! I always knew these people were untrustworthy and cunning. Hey you with the mustache! Get back in line. But sir, I am tired. You, you want to lie down? Linekeeper, help this man to lie down. It's time to leave. Close up. Have a safe trip. Ha!...Mr. Wentz, Mr. Wentz? I can't take it anymore. This torment. This nervous fear of mine! This shadow...this shadow...I was...Ah what a horrible dream! I am very glad it was only a dream. They are becoming all too common. I fear it portends things to come. Mr. Wentz. Yes, who is it? The landlord sent us up to repair the leak in your bathroom. Of course! But there is no leak. Oh, no! Colonel Herron, shall we do it or will you do the honorable thing? I will do it…only following orders…only following orders…The two men left in a hurry. It was almost sundown and the Sabbath would begin.

Republick

Well Tom, we certainly have ourselves a situation here. We sure do Johnny. Unlike any I have seen in any lifetime or any age. You date yourself, Tommy. You look as ragged as I do Johnny ole' pal ole' buddy of mine! We don't look a day over 50! Hmm. Speak for yourself. Okay. Okay. Not day over 49! Alright. That is enough. What about Georgie? Well what about poor old Georgie? We don't need him yet. But I told you anyway before we started this thing that he wasn't needed yet. Sometimes I am not sure that he is the guy for this. I see what you mean. There has been a lot of talk that his input may not be constructive or useful. We are looking at a few other guys who we may want to try out but no conclusion has been decided yet. So, for the time being, pencil him in and let's get going on the other parts. I am all ears Tommy boy! Righto Johnny! Hmm. Hmm. Let us see. Whatcha' thinking Tommy? We are looking for an old concept with new bangles. Glitter and gold? No. Something that is more simple and more basic. A thought or supposition that is as old as the universe itself. I get your drift. But it has been tried before by some of our predecessors. Unfortunately, too many deviations were encountered and complications arose that were not dealt with correctly or in most cases, too late. However, there were a few successes. You're right, Johnny. But the purity was short lived. That is always the case. Unfortunately, when dealing with imperfections, that is always so. Perhaps there are such blinkers on the creators of the structure that they cannot see the cracks of the foundation but only the massiveness and glory of the edifice. A certain lack of modesty or the thought of saying, "This thing is good." Or, "It is strong and it will last a millennia." It may last a billion eras but the foundation is full of fissures and cracks. The edifice itself can be whitewashed and its view held in high esteem. However, the key is the foundation. A strong foundation that yes, may have issues, but is constantly tended and cared for. But Tom, that is with all things. You are right, John. You are so right. So when one or many design and build a monument to a thought or concept, there must be an allowance for a little sway and give. A little stone or mortar or when the building decays beyond recognition, its total destruction. Yes, it may not be perfect but flaws and warts that are exposed can be removed or excised. That is a concept, Tommy, that should be in the hearts and souls of all civilized beings. Yes, a heavy thought, that must be borne for the good of all. Yes, the good of all. Now, Johnny try this on for size. Okay, Tommy, shoot. “We the people…”

Surreptitious

Good morning, George. Good morning, Willie. It is always a pleasure for our friends to drop by. George, better our friends than the ones wanting to come over. Bravo! My silver-tongued ally! May I light up? Willie, it is always alright for you to light up. There is so little time to relax these days. Unfortunately you are correct, George. And how is the Missus? Very fine spirits, thank you. And the children? As well as can be expected in these challenging times. I am in complete accordance with you on that. George, you have shown to be an excellent leader in your oratory and actions. All the ceremonial activities and speeches are a penny a dozen, but to encourage, and inspire, I am much weak at. You underestimate your own skills, George. A leader's job is to be, well, a leader. You are much beloved, George. No, Willie. It is you. You make these extraordinary speeches that draw people out and rally them to the cause. I may, but it is with your love and respect that I can do that. I am no power behind the throne. The throne's power is from the one who occupies it. Willie, you are a good friend and brother. So too, George. So, too. Now to business. George, have you been in contacts with your overseas friends? Yes, I have. And what have they told you? The same as last time. Wait. Wait. Be patient. Time will force an injection. I suspect, George, that this injection will be quite painful and will take many years to heal. Sadly to say, Willie. And from your contacts? Well George, it goes like this. Holding your hands up in the air and shrugging tells me the same thing: Don't call us, we'll call you. Correct, George. It seems that Frank is straddling both sides of the fence. He wants to, but sentiment expressed is opposed to. A very challenging position, Willie. For us, just the opposite. We have no choice since our very existence and glorious history depend on it. Frank has no issues like these. He is trying different ways to get his own house in order but cannot due to legal issues. I disagree with his methods, but his town is his and our town is ours. Not a good idea to interject ourselves since we need his help. You are correct, Willie. A message for you sir. Thank you, Thompson. It seems that our Eastern friends may have our answer and Frank knows that too. Yes, George. I have long suspected that these folks have the key to unlock the door. There have been quiet whispers that Frank has been looking to be on our side of the fence. Not out of friendship and commonality, but to render the negative economics dead and to maintain his current address. Very sad state of affairs. If things became bad, not just one person's address would change, but millions upon millions. Terrible! The fate of people is all dependent on the place where he lives and how much change he has in his pocket. Willie, I don't know. George, you must know. You and I and millions and millions unborn will know what happens today, tomorrow, and the days to come. Get hold of your thoughts, George and you and I will open the door to a world that will be forever changed. Things not at our expense but at the expense of the corrupted and unwashed. Yes, Willie. You are right. No, George. Both of us and the people waiting for us. Yes, waiting. Let's step outside and nourish with confidence and love to our fellow men. Ladies and gentlemen, may I present to you the King of England and Winston…

Training

Well I hope this one turns out more successful than the last one and the last one before that. We have had this conversation for at least two eras with the same hope and then finally, with the same failure. I feel like I am losing my touch with these things. It used to be so much easier in my younger days – right on the coin with each and every one. An occasional miss, yes, but that is to be expected. But look who we are dealing with M' Lord. We are dealing with imperfection. I know that. It is the nature but it is our nature to be better judges of that nature. I can appreciate your view, but it is ultimately my choice and as I can see from the most recent time, flawed. Perhaps you are weary of this constant sameness. The ad infinitum of our work. The circle with no end and no start. But, again, M' Lord, even beings of our mind must rest from these labors. Yes, we are of superior intellect and strength but even the strongest must rest. I am not sure of what you are saying but I fear you are bordering on the line of heresy and sense. I know you too well for we have been companions for many suns and I know that you speak what is in your heart and not what is anti-clerical. I only speak honestly and have only your saneness and strength at the apex of my thoughts. You think well. Perhaps after the next. NO! I think now would be the prescribed time for that rest. What would you suggest? Atop the highest peak? At the bottom of the sea? A visit to the coldest place? A trip to the warmest isolation? Sounds too grand? No my Lord. Not in the least. They are all at your disposal and can be gotten there at the lift of a finger or the whiff of a thought. That sounds so simple. Why could not I have come up with this before? Sometimes, the obvious is directly in front of my very face! Well, we think too deep and make things very complicated rather than as simple as one plus one equals two. No! We look for the grand calculation that must be the correct way because of its impressiveness. And we all say, "Of course!" However, we are knocked back on our heels time after time and still we persist that the broader view must be correct. Unfortunately, my Lord, and as well as you have always known, this is not the case. Of course. Of course.

Of co…WAKE UP SIR! Oh, yes. Very interesting. Samuel, please send in the gentleman. We have made him wait too long. This way. My pleasure to meet you President Lincoln. No! It is mine, Mr. Grant.

Triangle: Three Angles – One Conclusion

Angle One: Good morning, Eagle. Good morning to you, Albert. What is on my agenda for today? Eagle, there are new developments. Albert, there are never any new developments, just outgrowths and continuations. You are right, sir. It seems that the masses are moving in unison and with a defined cause and leader. Very good. Is it the leader who we think it is? Yes, it is, Eagle. And where is he now? He is in his home with his wife and children. A very humble and strong stage for what is to come next. Eagle, it is a natural setting for a man of humble means and a starting point. Remember, all politicians always go home after they have voted to do the family thing, Albert. That is true, regardless of how they vote either by the ballot box or the wooden box. Yes sir. Yes.

Angle Two: Good afternoon, Hawk. Good afternoon, Simon. Any further news? Yes, there is. Please pour yourself a cup of tea and begin this session. Yes, Hawk. Apparently within the last eight hours, a large and mobile group of the citizenry has proceeded from their workplace to the objective at point B4. They are moving as if their whole life depended on it. And as you know Hawk, it does. Very good. Carry on. Thank you. The person selected as who we thought would be, was. He is presently at his abode. Last time it was checked, he was having his dinner and smoking his pipe. From what we can also ascertain, in good spirits and confident in his outlook. Thank you Simon. What is next on our agenda?

Angle Three (The Apex): Good evening, Dove. Good evening to you and evening blessings. Amen. Yes, Amen. I hope that the thing we have prayed for will finally come true. I pray every single waking moment that all men may live the way that is unnatural to become natural. It is a moral and ethical way that the Divine has constructed our basics and mores. It grieves me beyond the pale that chains and lashes exist instead of roses and rainbows. I understand completely, Dove. I too, pray that this shall pass. It never will. As long as Satan is loosed from his cell, oppression and evil will rule over the hearts and minds of people. This, regardless of the strength or the wisdom of one. Yes, Dove. Yes. According to our information, the people are marching as a single heart and the warrior is at home with his family just waiting for the correct time. The correct time. The correct time. Remember, liberation has no wrong time. Yes, Dove. Yes. Amen my brother. Amen.

The Conclusion (Intersection): This is an important news brief. Within one hour ago, the communist government of Vichyland had fallen. It has been reported that the leader, Roytote Vinglass and his immediate bodyguards were surrounded at the winter palace and were arrested without incident. The crowds were chanting and cheering in a cacophony resembling a soccer game that was won by the home team. The supposed father of this coup, Gilresh Udine, was at his home reading and relaxing with his children and wife. No word on when he will make an appearance. In a joint communique, the President, Madame Prime Minister and His Holiness, the Pope....

The Jesus Chronicles

Faith

Sir, I am here. I know. You have shown to me that you have the message in your heart and soul. I am not so sure. As the day is long you do. One had to be chosen and it is you. Every person in life has a certain task, whether unpleasant or pleasant. Yours, my true friend, is neither. I am still not so sure. Your doubtfulness is your guide in this matter. Your strength underlies your flesh and will soon be exposed as true. It will be the only time in your existence that you can demonstrate this. After that, you will be cast as evil and your name not said. You will be scorned and scorned again by those who have their own ambitions. You will not fit the view as will be known. Those people are not true but have a larger agenda to corrupt and neatly fit a puzzle together of their own design. You, my friend, will be at the center of this grand mission. It will not be seen in the light but in the dark tabernacles of caves and few hearts. This will be your curse. I am so afraid and yet I am not. I know this thing will be done and must be done. That is correct. Without you, this will be just another bedtime story for children and old wives. I don't wish to be thought of as evil and accursed. Do not fear! There are many who will be remembered this way for what will transpire. You, me, and those others will be the closest to the truth as to the events that will transpose. Their fate and yours and mine will be so intertwined so as to create something universal that has never been or will be seen. It is truly, I say, that you will know more than any other living creature, including those today and those yet unborn. Friend, I believe what you say. I am not sure wholly, but I will. Yes, I know you know. There will be a split second that all will be revealed to you. And in that split second, everything will capture your heart and mind. I will believe. NO! I believe now in what has to be done. I know this to be true. I always knew this to be true from your inception to the last breath. Jealousy is a bad trait but our friends are at this moment are conniving bad history and legend about you. Truly, they know what has to be done but are more concerned about their own being and reputation. They fear the final blackness and the only thing between them and the finality is me. But for their lack of courage, they will pay the ultimate price. Not in their bed or quietly under the shade but a brutal and vengeful passing. Then, they will understand. You understand already. You know. It is time. Romans, here is your man. Here is the one who seeks rebellion and overthrow. Here is the man who is called the Chr…

Choices

Friend, I am a tired man. Yes, sir. You have been up since very early this morning, all this being today. And every day that has led up to today. Not just physically, but spiritually and mentally. Even with you going to worship services, a man can be tired, as he can be tired of living. You are much wiser than all the wise men that have ever existed. From the day the first sun shone long ago till the bleary of today. I am just a poor ole' man helping out another poor ole' man. A man who has the burden of the world on him. You make it seem so simple, Friend. So much more than if the sun rises today it must rise again tomorrow. Yes sir, it must. Why, Friend, must it? The laws of nature are fixed. The clouds expel water, a plant must grow, a person eats. Something we are taught on our grandfathers' knee or at the schoolhouses' wooden chairs. Friend, you speak so well. You are not only a Friend in the true sense of the world but a wise and learned sage. No, I have made a quick study of you and all others I have served for. The wisdom that you have has not amounted to more than a grain of wheat, but many grains and many sowings have given an insight that is as deep as the river that runs in the desert. Yes, Friend. I realize that I am not the wisest man and only serve at the behest of more powerful. Like others, I yearned for a position of glory and stature, but, no! I serve in a forsaken position in a forsaken land with for a forsaken people. I care much that I may have offended you with such comments but it is how I feel. I take no offense. I heard the same remarks before, before, and before that. My skin is deep and my blood runs cold. I grieve deeply, Friend, for my soul that I may someday may make a decision that is wise and not callous. A truly well thought out one based on the facts and fairness as opposed to sticks and coins. This is why I have pain today. I have never made an honest choice in my life and somehow, I feel this will be one. I feel a god is guiding my hand and soul toward something that is bigger than all of us. How history will judge me or what I do today is unknown but I must be as fair so as not to make a mistake. Is it destiny, my Friend? I believe that we were each assigned a book of life and it is ours to read it from end to end and skip not a word. Our role has been defined and we must carry it out. Like the match that burns down a farmers' field. It is bad that food had been destroyed and a man's livelihood canceled. But, the farmer soon discovers that it was good in that lurking in the grain buds were locusts. The gods of nature used a tool that in this case was good and the farmer was rewarded with a tenfold harvest. This, I feel, is your fate. Your day in the arena. Your day as a tool for the greater good. You will be seen as evil. However, without you…I have said too much. Go, make your decision. Somehow, Friend, I believe you. Guards, bring in that man. Citizenry, this man has done no wrong. Do as you wish. I wash my hands.

Family

I knew this day would have to come. Me too. I am having a great deal of difficulty in coping. That is completely understandable. You talk as if I had a bunion and you would say, “Put something in your shoe. You’ll manage.” I apologize for being glib and uncaring but we are in the same boat. We are all suffering in different ways: mother, children, aunts, uncles, and very close friends. Well where are the other supposed “close friends”? Huh? You mean cowards? We were told not to judge. But we all are human and getting into this situation required and will continue to require some value judgment. I believe you are correct but this frailty of ours will disappear and a better view of things should take its place. You women sound like philosophers or women chatting about the price of figs or fish. Most of us understand your situation. No you don’t! I am very insecure and simple minded. I shudder at the scampering of a mouse or a tree branch snapping. I am afraid of my own shadow. I sleep with the light on. Now, these fears are real. So, now women say words of comfort and solace or can you think of nothing more than “Oh well”? You were chosen and agreed to your role. No arm twisting. No beating with clubs. Just a mind as absorbent as sponge – soaking everything in and accepting the true message. You accepted this challenge with some hesitation. But great things always have a mental delay. We shall stay together. We shall cry together, we shall be happy together. And most all, share the warmth of this journey together. Well, yes…A stranger approaches. There are no strangers but companions in the truth, my love. Hello. Friend, there is no need to shield your face. You are amongst friends. Can you not speak? Do not be afraid? Can you not hear? Are you a leper? Your journey has taken you to the place of comfort and well-being. There is only love here. What matters is in your heart and soul and not the world view. Thank you but I cannot stay. I have duties to attend to. I feel very ill with discomfort and shame. I have had the world at my feet and now I feel as though a chasm has opened up and swallowed me whole. You are troubled much. But you too have been selected. There has been a hand guiding us all. One to do this. One to do that. And another to do that. From the consummation of time to the moment, a predetermination has existed that this must be done. If not us and not this time some others and some other time. My children, we must pray that this has not been in vain. You. I recognize you. That purple cloak. The ring. Aren't you…Yes, I am. I, too, have a key but my key is one of many. Not as sharp or golden as yours. But a key, nonetheless. I am ashamed but accepted my role as definitive and conclusive. I will be hated and scorned and misunderstood but will pass on and forgotten and my troubles will end when I turn to earth. Tears are all in our thoughts. Dry them. They will be needed no more.

To be continued with…

Faith…

Comfort

Hello and good morning. Hello, my loved ones. You slept with the lights off. You slept with comfort and serenity on your face. I do not feel rested. I twisted this way and that. I cried. I laughed. I died. A natural progression in these times. We have experienced each of us these emotions. As time ponders on we do less of each but death happens only once. And this death is a spiritual death. An end to confusion. An end to self-doubt. But a beginning to new perspective, a new awakening. And if we think that we die a thousand times, we are wrong! Falling ill is not merely a physical state but a soulful one at that. There are cures for the tangible but who is to say there isn't for the intangible? No, my son. You have died. There is no return from the abyss. So please my child, wipe your tears, quench your hunger and tend to the errand at hand. I am not hungry. Let us go now before the noon-day arrives. Please, each one of you take a basket and a good pair of walking shoes. Let us go. My child, what is the matter? I am indeed suffering much. How so? I feel very lonely and hated. A common thread here. And...But I was hated before and loved before. And what price love? A couple of coins or a loaf of stale bread. Then I was loved no more. This person was genuinely beyond all these things. I would have gladly given myself but was not asked. Pleasures of the physical body are passing but pleasures of the mind are continuous. I now understand this. And do not correlate both with each other. Enjoying the beauty of a rainbow. Enjoying the sound of a newborn babe. To this day, I carry that deep within my bosom. So, my child, we are all hated but we derive strength from hate...love from scorn...contentment from disillusionment...life from death. Thank you, mother. We are almost there. I do not care for this place. Neither do I. I feel as though I am picking out my own. Now, my loves, this is a place of joy and rest. A place that we cannot avoid. Besides, if not here, somewhere else? A cool shade tree? Or perhaps besides a quiet stream. No, my children. When we are branded on our feet, do we care where we lie? We cannot. The body decides and sleeps where we sleep. The outcome in each case is the same.

Excuse me. There is our friend a little behind us. Shall we wave to him? No. Each person must arrive at the finish line in their time. Ages will pass and the trophy will be waiting. We are here. Oh, my goodness! What malevolence!

Hope…

Journey

I cannot believe what I see. Is there nothing sacred! Thieves and scoundrels. May they rot in hell! Mind your tongue my loves. Have none of you been paying attention! Is a mothers' instinct at work here! No! No! And no! Have you been deaf? Have you no eyes? Have you no sense of a sweet and comforting aroma? Not in a basket on a lawn or in a farmers field. How about a basket next to your bed or the farmers' compost pile? Those are where you are at. You must remove yourself from the frailties of everyday living and step out of your doors to fragrances and honey. I do not wish to hurt you in any way but you were the closest. Comforted are those who are further away for their want is greater. Mother, I understand. I as well. Please forgive us. A mothers' duty is to scold, correct and love. This way the child's path becomes straight instead of tortured and gnarled. Wipe your tears my little ones and see. I see our friend is here. Have you secreted the...No, I have not! You have political motive and thoughts of self-aggrandizement. Haven't you understood your roles? It is as plain as the moon rising. I understand. You pretend to understand. You were present. You ate the same food. You shared the same friends. You were there at the beginning and now, at this place. I was none of these. I traveled a distance – physically and mentally. The trees were cleared one by one. Two by two. Until there were none. There was only grass and sunshine around you which afforded you an unobstructed view. You feared one day the tree would grow and mature and die. You could not see that! The blinders of ignorance were attached. But they were removed slowly and surely. Step by step. Day by day. Culminating at this time. It has all been revealed but you act like scared little children after a disturbing bed time story. "Mother, I am scared. Do not be frightened my little one. As you get older your fears will subside. And you will realize the difference between what is true and what is not true." You are this child. And you are awake. And still your confusions reign. Comforted are those not by their mother for their need is great. Come my children. There is a man sitting talking to somebody. Sir? Oh sir? There seems to be some type of great mischief here. Can you help? Yes. My journey is one of help. If something is misplaced, it will be found. If a child has strayed, safety will be his. If the grapevine is dying, it will be pruned. If a man is aching, a lawn of grass will be his. If one dies, he will have new breath. And, if one is thirsty, the spring will quench. Sir, we are most comforted by those words for we too, have been touched. And it has been I who has touched you. I stand now out of the shadows for you to see! Fulfilled are those who are empty for they shall have their fill! My mother. My broken woman who sold her body. My simple friend for though he be will be hated, fulfilled the need for eternal life. The man who passed judgment on me to allow the journey to begin. And others and others and others. Though they are not here they expand their vines and plant new seed. Plant. Grow. Cultivate. Nurture. Fulfilled are the gardeners for theirs is the wheat!

Love.

Grassmere

I am much troubled. Why? Theory, conjecture, speculation, and all that is contained in that stew. We are not talking about food. In a sense, we are. That is why this is such an important thing. What happens when we wake? Perhaps we dream of a sweet fruit and take from the bowl a peach or apple. We look and say, "This will be good. I will feel quenched." Can we be wrong? Most likely not since past history indicates otherwise. We bite it, chew and swallow. The act continues until but only the core is left. We leave the core for the mare or rodent. It is bitter and hard to eat. In this case, the same can be said. The outside presented to us is inviting and filling and the core shows itself to be just a home for maggots and rot. That is the dilemma – sweet and barren or sweet and fruitful? I see your point but this is a special time. I disagree with your theory. As each moment progresses, it is a special time. Special at birth, two seconds later, 14 minutes later, 50 years later and the dark cloak. Special, special and more special. That is why we must be so, so sure. I retell and retell again: fruit and generation. I see your point. The proof is in the base not the meat. Is that your thinking? Yes, it is. We must delve to the center to see if it is worth our while. Must not we eat the meat to get to the core? Not necessarily. The expression "Rotten to the core" may not apply. Corruption, worms, rot, disease can be present but we must strive for the center – the seeds of existence and the fertility of future generations who will have no meal but the stuff that makes up our very being. I understand what you say and I greatly fear what you say has already come to pass. I see it in your face and hear it in your words. But truly I say, you have seen, now touch so that you can believe. The greatest believers are those yet come for they have only the core and you have both. In me, is the meat of sustenance and the marrow of faith. I see and feel. You do Thomas. You do.

Advice to Clergy

Blintzes

Good afternoon, Myron. Hulo, Rabbi Murphy. Whoever thought a rabbi could have an Irish name! It is an interesting story. However, our goal here is not to discuss genealogy but you Myron. Besides, you always ask the same question and I always give you the same answer. Pardon me young teacher, I always say it in a rhetorical way. It is not meant as a direct question but as an antidote for your lack of humor and dry lectures. Too, remember I am a very old man, very old. Anything that can cheer me up from the same old day after day. So please Rabbi, let's begin. Hmm. Okay. Let's begin. Let's see. Where did we leave off last time? Here we go. "And Moses came down from the mountain..." Those were the days...I...Myron, you interrupted me, again. Oh am I so sorry teacher. Just a little reminiscing. About what? Oh, you know. In my younger days I was quite active. I used to climb mountains, go for very long walks with my family and friends. Sometimes we would get arrested for vagrancy. Most of the time, as luck would have it, we escaped and started all over again. A vicious cycle but we had to persevere to be who we wanted to be. To do the things we wanted to do. To live. To breathe. To climb the highest peak or descend into the lowest depth. That is what Moses demonstrated by going up the mountain and then, coming back down. It was no Jack and Jill story. Trust me. But I groan on. Please young Rabbi, continue with your monotones. Being just out of Yeshiva you should be young and fresh and full of mental vigor. So, please go on! Myron, you never cease to amaze me. There are some things you are not taught but learn as the years go on. I feel all the semesters and all the lectures and all the projects can never add up to personal experience. You, my kosher and crusty old man have provided me with new insights and a sense of being. I may think some of your stories are a bit out there, but there must be some grain of truth lying deep within the cobwebs of your overgrown weeds of imagination. Rabbi, you are a very funny young man. You say I exaggerate, but can you prove otherwise. Were you there? Were you watching as me and my friends troll-oping about? Were you the sheriff who sent out his goons to rough us up? Young Rabbi, please forgive the rantings of an old man. It is all I have. The thoughts, the rantings, the ravings of an old man are all old men have. So please forgive me for I am old and lonely. Say no more, Myron. No apology is needed. All the lectures and all the semesters and all the visits to Temple can't make up for first hand experiences of a single human being. How about for a group of people – men, women, children and their four-legged creatures. Yes, Myron, for all those too! All add up to one. We must be ourselves. To be relatively free within the confines of a just and moral society. To be able to set out on our own and learn for ourselves. Be yourself! Be free! Be able to go up to the mountain and come back down. Or never go up but fall into a deep crevice. You eventually come back out but have you learned anything? Moses and his friends were in a deep hole but they climbed out, went up and back down. And they learned. Myron, you talk as if you were there. Young Rabbi with an Irish name and soul full of knowledge, I was.

Aesculapius

Bless me father for I have sinned my last confession was uh, uh, hmm. Was when my son? I don't really remember. What do ya' mean you don't remember? You must have recollection when you asked for forgiveness. Father I always ask for forgiveness and strength when I get up in the morning and when I go to bed. My son, that is good of you to do that. It is the Christian thing to do. But I mean when was your last formal confession to a confessor? Can't we just go on with my sins without the time and date of my last confession? Unfortunately not. It is in the book that you say that. It' s all part of this forgiveness thing. What book? The Bible? Nope. The book of rules and regulations of the Church. You know, like no meat on Fridays in Lent and not eating a meal before you receive Communion. And so forth and so on. Oh, I see. Alright, I got it. Okay my son. When was or when do you think you had your confession? Father, you are not going to believe this. Son, it's all procedural at this point. Trust me. I have heard everything from five minutes ago to 50 years ago. So not a thing you put out there will knock me over. Go on. My knees are killing me. From your own penance Father? That's enough! I'm listening to you not the other way 'round. Get on with it! I don't think I like the tone of this conversation, padre. Don't call me a padre. Do I look like I'm wearing a sombrero? Do you want me to answer for you or should we get on with the business at hand? Insolent! At this rate you may have to be asking for forgiveness at the end of a red-hot poker administered by a horn ridden fellow! Hmm. Whom are you working for oh wise confessor? Are you in league with Satan or the one who keeps you working? That my son, is enough from you. We can get on with this or I'm leaving so I can have my dinner and watch some cheesy soap opera. Now which is it? Perhaps cheese and crackers or a cheese soap opera is more appealing than the salvation of my soul. A theologian are we! It is true I have done some studying in my time and a little caring and consoling and hand-holding in the heaviest of times. Also, at the saddest times of farewell or at the beginning of living have I been there. Not as a friend, but as a voice. You might say a voice in the wilderness that shouts out to make a path. A path that leads out of the forest. A path to freedom. A path to one's own soul. No detours. No barricades. No blockages. When we get stuck and can't advance, we must act as our own healer and excise this tumor and cast it off to the pigs at the trow. The swine. The snakes. The bottom dwellers of our own nothingness. The unnamed one. Yes Father, I have sinned. My last confession was thirty years ago. Yes, I have had others, but that was the last meaningful one. The last real cleansing before I lay down in front of the Tabernacle and professed my heart and soul and body to Holy Mother Church. My marriage to Her. Yes Father, our last confession was thirty years ago.

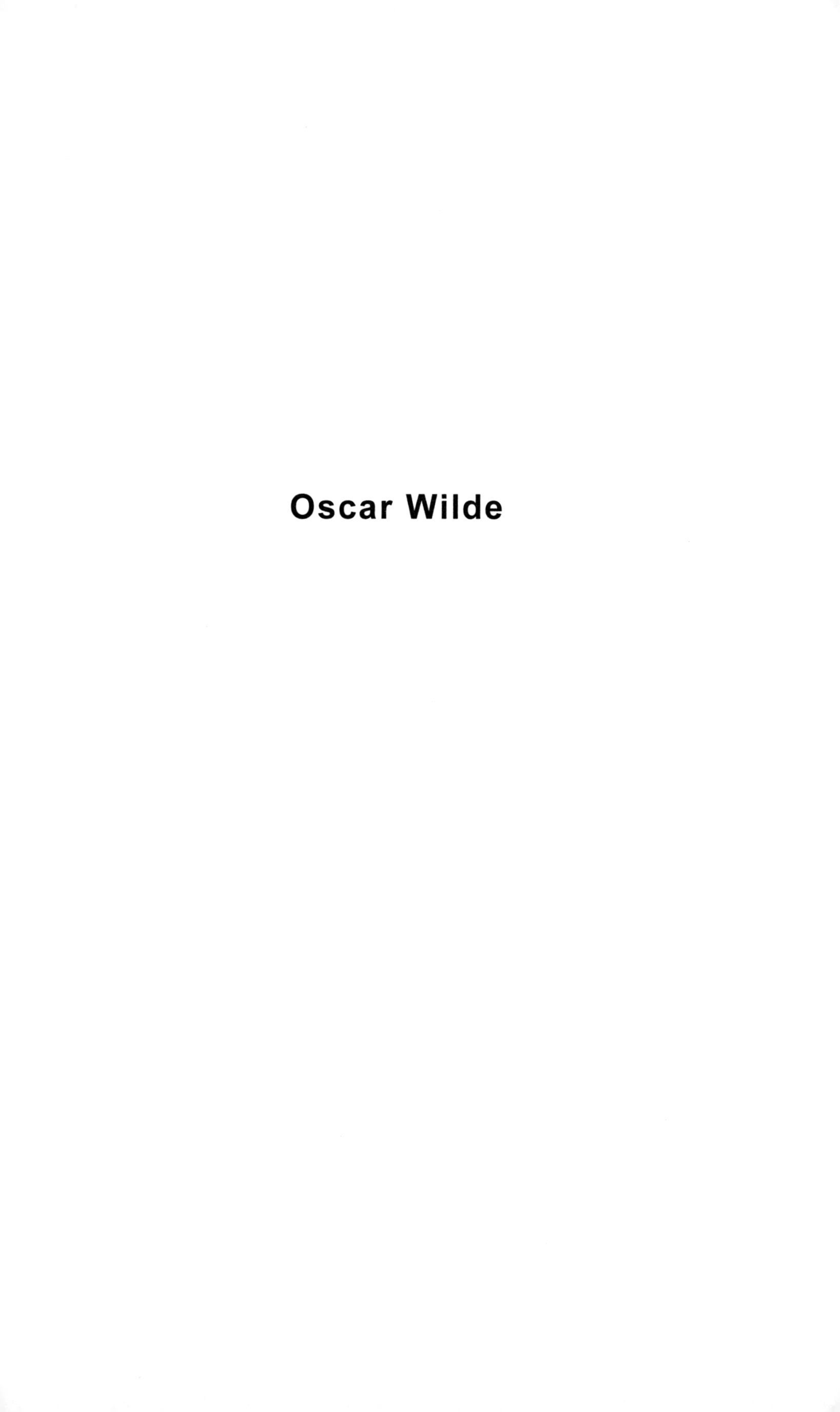

Oscar Wilde

Ad Hoc

Ladies, please welcome to the biweekly Tuesday Afternoon Tea and Emergency of the Week Auxiliary and Antique Club meeting. Bravo, Miss Crumple! Thank you, my dear cousin Ethel. And to all the other fine ladies who are here and who are not here, I say with a hearty, tsk tsk. Your voice will not be heard on the most treacherous issues of the day. Miss Crumple, you mean just to those who are not here? Oh, yes. My poor eloquence strangles my most simple thoughts. My extreme apologies Mrs. Clayrimple. Accepted Miss Crumple. We understand the loftiness from which you have to come down from. My modesty prevents me from disagreeing with you. Now with all that taken care of, what is on our agenda Madame Secretary, Miss Thimble. Thank you, Madam Chairwoman. Let me see. There is so much to consider with so little time. Absolutely correct Miss Thimble. At half past, there will be an emergency meeting of the Fine Arts and Crayon League. Our resident starving artist, Mr. Wickshamble, seems to have run out of supplies for his latest project – nude fig leaves. Oh my! Fret not ladies. Mr. Wickshamble says until he gets what he needs, he will place a non-descriptive washcloth over the offending parts. I knew we could trust that man. The finest that money could buy. But we never paid him anything. That is correct, Miss Balmorton. I keep insisting that we did and he simply misplaced the bank check. Brilliant Miss Crumple! How did you come up with that? Very complicated thinking. The process that was employed which would take many minutes to explain. Of course, Miss Crumple. Of course! As you know, our dear beloved pastor, the Right Reverend Dr. Hufnagel passed to the pearly gates some two weeks ago. It has come to my attention as the official sexton of our parish that a new pastor will be coming our way. We understand him to be fresh out of divinity school, 29, and eager to spread the word of our beloved Savior. His name is...is...my goodness I seem to have misplaced it. Oh here it is. It was in my right shoe so as to comfort me from a bunion on my large toe. We will make this quick since my toe is acting up. His name is the Reverend Mr. Greenwich from New South

Egregious. And this is the reason I have called you together this eve. It seems that the good reverend is a single man. We cannot have a man of God thinking about impure things especially while preaching a sermon on the unsheathing of guards' swords. Definitely not! Absolutely! Therefore we must find a suitable partner for the good Reverend. Perhaps Mrs. Whitcomb's daughter. She is very old for the reverend. Yes. I fear you are right. Elsie is twenty-four. An old maid just aging into oblivion. Here here! Miss Crumple? Yes, Ethel? How about Mr. Walcott's daughter, Bernice? He is a widower and needs her to go. It's been five years now and Mr. Walcott has been taking longer and longer walks. He seems to be pent up and needs a release. Absolutely Ethel! Bernice will be notified that her new chapeau is ready and she must pick it up before it goes to goodwill. Brilliant, Miss Crumple! Astounding! Thank you, ladies. You are too kind! What's this? Thank you, Burble for this note. You can go now. Oh my goodness! Pray tell Miss Crumple! Please hope it is nothing serious. I am afraid it is. It seems that the telegraph office made a mistake in transmitting the information about our new pastor. He is not a fresh 29, but an old prune of 92 and was castrated while doing a baptism at the River Rouge. It seems that there was a piranha accidentally released into the stream and the dumb fish thought that goose eggs had fallen into the water. Shall we cancel the meeting with Bernice? NO WE WILL NOT! In case you didn't know, Bernice is a nurse at the local hospice. She can help soothe the old man's ego.

Periwinkle

Oh what a lovely day! Yes, indeed Miss Francis. What color should I wear today? Oh, Miss Francis you look good in all colors and your choice of powder and eyeliner are always perfect. You flatter me, Hanna. Now, put aside all that you have said and help me pick out a color. If you insist, Miss Francis. Yes, I do. But first, the solutions for my fingers and finger tips. Oh, yes, I almost forgot to tell you Miss Francis that the Eau de Crepe mixture that you purchase has been discontinued at Howard's. Oh, no! Not Eau de Crepe! Did you go to Williams Fine Toilette? I did go there but they only had very little of it left and it was reserved for Mrs. Glenwinkle. That old cow! She has the taste of a dead frog and a hairstyle to match. How about Warren's Fine Sprinkles? Mr. Speck said he will try go find a distributor who may have some left but offered something called "An Ode to Eau". Speck is a deceitful bald little man with crooked teeth and business ethic to match. I am sorry for you Miss Francis. Shall I trek down to Wallougbie's. He always seems to come up with beauty needs that are hard to find. No, Hanna. No. I shall have to find another mixture that will suit my delicate and fine textured fingers. But, I will put aside this temporary sadness and attend the matter at hand. Yes, Miss Francis. Now, the color of the day. Perhaps a powder blue outfit with a splatter of white daisies down around my knees. Miss Francis, a perfect color to match the outside! Blue for the sky and the white daisies as clouds! Of course, but I wore that last Tuesday when I attended a reception for the new vicar. A crumpley old man who reminds me of a Papist in disguise. All his talk of giving everything to the poor. But, mam...Yes Hanna. You are right. That is the injunction the good Lord gave us. But, ooh, I hate those Pope lovers. He wears white everyday – no matter what season it is. He is not only money poor but good taste poor. Yes, Miss Francis. No, Hanna, no. I think a bright red outfit with a bright red hat and an umbrella to match would make the day. Red? I never thought of it. Did you not just wear it? I did about two weeks ago at the ambassador's reception at the Hotel Grunion. So, but will anybody notice it? I don't think so.

The ambassador was color blind. Good choice, Miss Francis. Okay, Hanna. Someone is at the door, Miss Francis. Well, don't just stand there! Go get it Hanna. It might be something important, like an invite to Miss Tweed's daughter's engagement party. Miss Francis, you will never believe this. What Hanna, what? Mr. Ballfore of Twiddle's Fine Tea and Cosmetics Shop heard of your dilemma from Mr. Speck and has sent over his personal supply of Eau de Crepe for your personal use and at no charge. No charge? Mr. Ballfore is a creepy man who tries to get me to go to the opera with him but I refuse. Mr. Ballfore does not strike me that way, Ma'am. I think he has other motives. Miss Francis? He wishes to corner the market on sea salts from the River Glunk in Germany and sell it to me at inflated prices. No other reason, but let us move on. Yes, Miss Francis. Oh, that feels so good, Hanna. Some more hot water but not too much. Yes. That does it! One or two minutes is all that it takes. I am off. See you at noon for cucumber sandwiches and crumpets. Yes, Miss Francis. Hanna, my lovey. Yes? You are such a smart little girl! I get that from my upbringing from a fine ole' wheezer of a dad like you. Hook, line and sinker dear old pop? No, my little lovely girl! Hook, line and stinker!

Tiddlywinks

Miss Brewster, are you in? And who is looking for Miss Brewster? Her sister Mrs. Armbruster. Oh, just a minute to see if she is in. My Lady, your sister is here. Do you wish to see here or are you in dispose? Yes, tell her I'm in the Meadows Sanitarium having my gallbladder checked. Okay my Lady. Mrs. Armbruster? Yes? Your sister has had a medical emergency and is having her liver, I mean gall bladder examined. Tell my beloved sister that this is the 14th time she has had her gallbladder checked. Mention to her that if she is to have some of her anatomy examined, there are plenty more to go around and she should pick something less important, like her brain. I will convey to your sister your deepest regards for her health. Good day, Mrs. Armbruster. Good day to you and your witch of a mistress! Your right, Lillian, I should pick a more important organ to demonstrate how ill I really am. Perhaps my esophagus or my urinary tract. I think that would be a very good idea, my Lady. Yes, Lillian. Yes. Is Mrs. Wingate coming by today? No, my Lady. She has a flareup of her gout and is bedridden. She sends her deepest apologies and hopes to visit on the second Tuesday After Full Moon Tea and Cucumber Saturday gathering. Too much liver, I suspect is causing her discomfort. Call Dr. Purdy and have him visit Mrs. Wingate at my expense. The fine doctor is an expert on gout and severe acne. Yes, my Lady. Miss Walters, when will she be coming by? Didn't she say about noonish? Yes, my Lady. However, I received a short note from her Aunt Eloise that the pretty young thing broke her leg while playing croquet. How painful! It seems that Miss Walters was picking a daisy and the ball struck her quite nicely on the kneecap. She was taken to Saint Elmo's Fire Hospital and will be there a few days. Awful! Poor girl! She is just turning 18 and at this rate, will be an old maid by the time she is 22. Send her a note with my sympathies and tell her she should pick a hobby more indoorish, like checkers or finger painting. Yes, Ma'am. Canon Reverend Sykes should be here soon. Unfortunately, my Lady, the good Canon will be unavailable to show up. Why not? It seems that there was an emergency on the

Old Lane Road involving a fish truck and a group of Buddhists. Surely, the good Canon did not give solace to the heathens. I pray tell he did. He explained that we are all God's children, whether we deliver clams and shrimp or sit like pretzels on a floor mat. Hmm. Sounds heretical to me. Perhaps so my Lady. My dear Lillian, what is on our schedule for this noon? A trip to the races, but the stewards called of the races due to an epidemic of locust harassing the poor horses. Two of the poor beasts escaped and caused the collision between the believers and non-believers I just told you about. Oh! very unfortunate. Yes, indeed my Lady! Well, my Lillian, I believe that about clears our schedule for today. Yes, my Lady. What shall we do? I think I will take a nap and plan for tomorrow's activity. You must continue your project. The ones with the leaves? No. The recipe book that we are putting together. Yes. The name? It is "One Hundred and One Ways to Entertain Your Guests".

Sherlock Ohms

Ohms – The Case of the Missing Otatoe

Come in Knutson. Ohms, you never cease to amaze me. I know. Pray tell did the ife take away our favorite ottle pener? Thank Od, no! Then what is it as if I didn't already did not know. It was my lucky olf's oot. The old ow mashed it under er inosaur eet and ate it. Ate it? Yes, Ohms. Ate it. As an og swallows a one in one ulp, so did the ife down it – ur and all. Obviously, unlucky for the oth of ou. However, Knutson, be glad ou are rid of it. Our uck should become better or at least neutral. Pray that the ife suffers the same ate as the olf's oot. Bravo, Ohms! Bravo! Knutson, please make ourself comfortable. The ookah is primed and ready to go. Much obliged Ohms. I have a pair of fine ocks that I use when I go olfing. Always make ar and an occasional irdie. I am envious, Ohms. Again, ou should be. Oh, Knutson, please get the oor. We have a isitor. And I can tell by the ootsteps, a an heavy set and bald. Bald? Yes bald. Otherwise, the ootsteps would be slightly heavier. Ohms Ohms Ohms! The oor the oor the oor. Well look here. It is Permutter from Lub 34. Ohms, set aside the ntroductions and help me with my roblems. Permutter, can't ou see it is late and Ohms needs is rest. Come back omorrow when e can properly ignore ou. Knutson, enough of the outhings and enjoy the ipe. Pshaw Ohms. Pshaw. So, Permutter our 129ilemma. Ohms, thank ou for telling Knutson to stand down…I am warning ou Permutter. A proper hrashing is what ou need and I am the one to do it! Again, Knutson, enjoy the ipe or I shall chop off our oot and feed that to our lovely ride. Hmm. Sorry for the nterruptions and go on. Yes. The symbol of the lub is missing. Which is…The otatoe. My ord Permutter. That is surely a risis indeed. Can you help me, Ohms? Yes, I can. But Ohms…I am warning you, Knutson. Sorry, ole hap. Carry on Permutter. When was it discovered missing? This orning half past ight. Hmm. I have it! Simple as the ose on our ace. Ha ha, Permutter. Simpley hideous and obtuse! Alright, Knutson, to the nteroom and wait for me there. It will be the purple andanna for oday! Yes, Ohms. Sorry, Ohms. Too late. For ou Permutter, the nswer is simple. A ea. Yes a ea. Huh? You see my sad riend, omeone is playing a horrid rick on you. Me? Yes ou. Why not the entire Lub? That is for another ime. Okay Ohms, please carry on. Indeed. A ea is the rux of this roblem. Omeone who will remain nameless scrawled the etter on the sealed ase in order to cause ou much istress. Isn't that right, Knutson? I fear, yes, Ohms. But it was meant to be a rank in the fine spirit of ommaradery and riendship. Obviously not, Knutson. Obviously not. At this very moment Permutter, the offending symbol is being removed and ou shall have our Otatoe back. How can I ever repay ou, Ohms? We are using the purple or should I say, the urple andanna this venning and a good ound would certainly cheer ou up. Erhaps another ime. Good night, Ohms. Good night you wine, Knutson. Or should I say: Oink oink! Hmm. Get ome safe and send y egards to table 15 Ermutter.

Ohms – The Case of the Crunchies of the Baskerbilles

Knutson, how was surgery today? Oh, the usual nonsense, Ohms. For example, if I may? Go right ahead, Knutson. Mrs. Claydimple came in today complaining of an extreme pain in her right hand, I looked and noticed that she inadvertently sown a sock on her hand while fixing a very nasty hole. Did you amputate? The hand or the sock? Never mind, Knutson. Carry on. While removing the sock, I noticed that she had sown the sock on so well that I decided to sign up for one of her sewing classes to help me in my own poor suturing. Lesson learned. For who, my dear chap? None of the above. Oh by the way, answer the door, Knutson. The…Oh never mind! Witherspoon, what is matter? I just came back from the lowlands. And…No need to continue, Witherspoon. What is all this then about the lowlands? You see, Knutson, there is this legend that when one goes there, they never return. And why my dear Ohms? The crunchies. The what? The crunchies! While walking in the lowlands you gradually start to hear a crunching sound – as the legend goes. It gets louder and louder as you go deeper and deeper. All this until…well you get the idea, Knutson. Blimey! On our way to the lowlands, my dear, Knutson. What about Witherspoon? He is in the kitchen munching on something. He is safe here. Time is pressing, Knutson. Hmm. Ah. Hmm. Da di da. Here we are. The High Road to the lowlands. There it is, Ohms. See! I knew it. Let's keep walking, Knutson. The noise is becoming deafening, Ohms! Let us leave! Oh put away the child and let the man show, Knutson. Sorry, ole' man. I forgot. Forgiven. But I do have the answer. Tell me, Ohms. Tell me! Sit down on this log and I shall tell you. But first, listen. By Jove, Ohms. The noise has stopped. Aye! Quite elementary my dear, Knutson. As we first entered the lowlands, there was no sound. So far so good. Once we started walking, the crunching sound began. As we got further in, the noise became deafening. Absolutely my dear Ohms. Once we stopped to sit, silence was the rule. Come to think of it, that's right! You see Knutson, the ground became gradually harder as though we were walking on cement. And according to my keen intellect, it was. Huh? You see my dear colleague, the local health district decided to build a hospital here. Eventually it was built but sank and crumbled some 16 years later. With it, some 20 or thirty patients. And the crunchies are the souls of the patients? Please Knutson, there goes that child again. Sorry, Ohms. So, the cement. What did you have for breakfast, Knutson? Well, not the usual eggs and toast but Corn Crunchers because the grands came over for a couple of days and I thought I would be a good role model. Precisely! I knew that already in between your mustache and nose, are several crunchers now residing. Ooh! Ohms. Why didn't you tell me sooner? I needed a good laugh after I battled with Socrates and Plato and their dry intellect. Also, check your shoes. Ah! I thought they just needed some mink oil. You see, Knutson, the crunching sound was the sound of Corn Crunchers on the bottom of your shoes. Hence! And Witherspoon? He has 14 children and is the President of the Rice and Beans Cereal Company. You mean…Yes, Knutson – the maker of Corn Crunchers and other assorted noisy food. Blimey! But what about the legend? It was made by his competitors, the egg and bread industry. Whoa! Let's go back to Butcher Street. And one more thing, Knutson. Yes, dear chap? Wipe your shoes before you go in or I will disappear. Ha, Ohms! Ha!

Ohms – The Case of the Wrong Wishy-Washy

My my my! What is the matter, Ohms? This item in the evening paper. Tree rot at the Old Bailey's gardens? Much more severe than that. Really, Ohms. Yes really, Knutson. It says here that the price of this paper is going up a penny. Horrid, Ohms. Horrid. Shall I cancel the subscription? No need to. You see, we don't have one. I merely send one of the ragamuffins around to the trash bin and he scoops one the papers that has a tear or some other unfortunate malady. And how much do you pay him? Half a penny. It all makes sense, economically of course. How so, Ohms? Since the price of this tabloid has gone up a penny and I pay out a half, I come out even more ahead and now by one more penny. Brilliant, Ohms. Brilliant! Of course. Yes, come in. Well hello, Dillson. Ohms. May I borrow one of your evening shirts. Why, yes. The matter? You see, I sent this out to be cleaned and it got mixed up with a blue shirt and here we are. By Jove! You are right. Although the stain gives a pleasant and artistic look…Ohms! Please, no joking! I am having dinner with Lord Schnapps and I must look my best. You seem to be the fancy of the club set. Ohms, it is a curse but I shall endeavor. Well, Knutson, fetch one of mine. You know where they are. Right way! Lord Schnapps today. Lord Walker last week. Lord Rummy before that. And so on and so forth. Oh thank you, Knutson. Much better. Shall not keep you any longer. Have a good night, Dillson. And to you my fine fellows! What a character! Harmless. Jovial. Pleasant. Color blind. Color blind? You see Knutson, Dillson and I have this little bet that either one of us can win. I could but my modesty…Okay Ohms. Enough of the flattery. Yes. Cough. Cough. You see, I am as well color blind, but only in my right eye. Rare but true. Continue Ohms. In a nutshell, my dear Knutson, Dillson sees a stain and wishes it gone. And I bring out a new shirt and it is gone. But Ohms, the shirt I brought out had a red stain. Correct. In a day or two Dillson will notice the blotch and we start the cycle all over again.

Dillson is one of God's more simple creatures. No fuss. No muss. Just lots of bleach and hope. Something we all should strive for, Knutson. Yes, Ohms. Yes.

Philosophy, Morals, And Everything Else

5 = 5

The inverse to the polarity is equal to one-half the amount of pi reduced by one-third on or about the seventh day off the cycle except when the quarter half is in a dynamic ratio of three to seven as indicated by the prelude to the acrobat zenith except if the quarter indicator is in the frost stage, only if the phase is in the third middle-time of the ninth division. Are you sure? I believe so. This only if all things are equal. You are too precise and specific. Life is uneven and lumpy. The only thing that is constant is the unconstantness and unruliness of our existence. The plans set forth cannot be extrapolated from yesterday to today precisely for that lumpiness of our existence. There are things that are equal. Like five equal five? No! But five is five! For one must be first and one must be last. None are equal but are the same. My head spins at your logic! Your inverse ratios and so forth and so on only work when you are dead and buried! My complete thought in a thimble is this: be the first when being equal to your tasks!

Alicewhite

Wilhelm, speak to me. About what? The world. The world? Yes, the world! Quite a lofty and extensive topic and it might take a few minutes. I have all the time I need. You have always been a source of knowledge and strength. Perhaps even a quip or two. The only one who I might say is worldly enough. I am no philosopher or teacher or instructor but just a mere person WHO EXISTS just like you. No, not just like me otherwise I would not be asking you, Wilhelm. Touché! But what do you want to know and where would you like to start? Where a circle begins. You trouble me with your delight and depthness. Perhaps I should be asking you. Your mind is already awash with "isms" and I fear if anymore would cause you great distress. Wilhelm, you worry too much about things. Minds can expand but never contract. If we contract, we are dead. Maybe not bodily, but of wisdom. Ignorance is borne and the world stops. We become the primordial slop of our past and sink ever deeper. No lifeline. No rope. No hope. No nothing. The leprosy of the mind sets in and we become content to live in a colony of disease and separation. We live with others who also are content in this altered state. Ask the question: Who are you? Answer: I am the living dead. Warts. Marks. Pus. All. I am shunned by the wise and clean. Content to live with the same. Let the dead bury the dead. But at least I am warm and dry and with others. Wilhelm, I cannot live like that. I constantly fear I am sliding toward that slope and must be inoculated against ignorance and bliss. Wilhelm, again, please be my doctor and I your patient. No. No. Your own anti-bodies of your soul are in full operation already and all I must do is provide bandages and warm soup. Like a circle you will have no end but have always begun.

Astrid

Come here my child. Yes, mama? How are you spending this wonderful afternoon? I was in the garden chasing the butterflies and playing with the cat. You are a very talented little girl to be able to do all those wonderful things at once. Well mama, not at once. Sometimes I was chasing the yellow butterflies and when there were no more, I chased the kitten. And when I caught the kitten, the butterflies came back and we started the game all over again. And when, my child, the kitten ran away and the butterflies flew off, what did you do? I always go to the one who is always there – my mama! You are such a wonderful child! All mamas should have little girls like you! And all little girls should have mamas like you! Did you wish to know anything else about my day? No, my little one. You may go off to play and be back for dinner. Yes, my mama…My beloved husband…My beloved wife. You seem teary eyed my sweet. I am. She is so sweet and innocent and dread when she grows up she will no longer be the child that we will always know. Consider this my wife: Our girl is like a tulip. She blooms each season and with the winter, retires to her bosom to come back the following stronger and older. Her leaves are healthy and her bloom shines ever brighter. But one day, a creature may dig her up out of her comfortable ground – perhaps our little kitten – and be planted somewhere else. And the butterflies shall feed off of her nectar and they too will grow strong. In this she shares her nourishment with all, not just the garden of her birth and the soothing grasses. She will grow up and plant herself in the hearts of many but will always have the earth of our hearts. This is written in stone and carved in the oak. In this, she will never LEAF us – pardon the metaphor my love. You are forgiven my wise husband for you are of humorous nature and strong as a willow. My sweet day lily you shine every brightly at night and as well as the day!

Busy

Welcome home, Venetia. Glad to be back, Sinuso. How was your trip back? You know, the usual delays of what is this or how much did that cost or what is in that vial. You're right. There is no trust anymore. It can be understood but we had nothing to do with that thing. After all, that was over 375 vignoods ago. I suppose Venetia, that is the way of all things. But be that as it may, I have a wonderful blarshset up for you. You do? Thank you so much for a blarsh, Sinuso. My pleasure. All my other 32 partners could not appreciate things the way you do. I cannot see why, Venetia. Also, I have another surprise that you might like. Tell me, Sinuso! Pretty please with an eggblard on top? You are very close! It is something I picked up at B'nooshs'. And pray tell what is it? Yellow matter custard covered in noobglarbs. Glarbs! I love glarbs! Domestic or imported? Only the best. Hand rolled from the fields of Tubo. Sinuso, you are a bad boy! Not bad for 126! You act like a boy of 53! Venetia you are too kind and generous. Here, let me help you with your luggage. What's this? What is what? This purple vial and the chip that says "Nimnom"? Actually, it is none of your business. We are not legal or anything like that. Besides, we are only in a stage one relationship. I am under no obligation…Whoa Venetia. I was just asking. Please calm down! I am sorry, Sinuso. These long trips always get the best of me. Please forgive me, Venetia. Forgiven. Now, let me get changed and washed and I will be right out. Sinuso to Barga, please. Yes, it is here. Yep. Hmm. Hmm. Very good. Out. You were talking to who, Sinuso? An old pal way back to the academy who I just…Just what, Sinuso? Now, there you go again. Your paranoia is startling me, Venetia. Sinuso or is it Osunis? You are not too bright in hiding your true identity. Just as your name is backward, so is your thinking and your entire way of life. You were looking at the vial of purple liquid and the chip. The vial first. You see, the vial is nothing but juice from an oblogoth tree. Simple, basic stuff. The true stuff of life. Venetia, ouch! Oh look there, Osunis. You are bleeding purple. Isn't it supposed to be clear? Everybody's blood was synthesized to a clear color so as not to be alarming and distressing. Same cells and same everything but color. All a mind game. However, me and my brethren were able to change it back to a purple. Not quite red, but close enough. The original formula was lost but is close to achievement. Your friend Barga is here. Say hello Barga. A nibnu bird! As you know, nibnu birds are very smart and can take instructions well. A genius like you fooled by a fine feathered creature. You idiot! But Venetia? But nothing! I disliked you from the very start! You twerp! You vile round bag of ignoo pus! You were so taken by me that you did everything but ingest my soul. And that is not for sale. The chip is a sacred relic that contains the origins of all things. Red blooded things. Red blooded from the top to the bottom. The redness that defines what is to be human. And the soul? Well the soul can never be changed. Your exterior may be bruised and damaged but the very soul is the last bastion of one's self. The corrupted can be restored and rescued and the exterior be bandaged and healed. But the soul will never be changed and the purple blood of weakness and deceit will eventually be changed to the redness of strength and pure intent. Osunis, the face of you is now turning crimson and your blood is now the same. Welcome home.

Carpetbaggers

How did we wind up in a place like this? Like where? Here? Where is here? Where is HERE! You tell me! You brought us to this, this mud laden dirt hole. Oh, yes, yes. I remember. We're in a place called, called, uh. Hmm. Desousa? No. NO. Azusa. Yes! Yes that is it! Azusa! Now why are we here? Now you you! I have had just enough of this double-talk. One day we are here and the next day we are there. One night we are walking down Highway 232 and the next we are the guest of fifty stinking and squealing pigs. Yeah, that was tough. Couldn't stop thinking about bacon and eggs for a whole week. Yeah, all that bacon and eggs got us was three-day old cheese sandwiches and heartburn. And I can still taste that crunchy stuff. I think it was mayo. Mayo is not supposed to be crunchy. My filling almost fell out. Now! You! What is next Einstein? I must ponder that thought carefully as I sit and look around for a nice and comfy hole in the ground where I may contemplate such weighty issues. The only weighty issue is going to be my size eleven weighty shoe against your air-filled balloon that resides over your weak-kneed shoulders! No threat of violence is going to solve anything. Okay. You smash my head into a billion molecules of oxygen and you wind up with a foot full of sawdust, being homeless, hungry and completely baffled by everything but of our own desperate situation. Snore. Wheeze. Cough. Cough. Argh. It is cold. Where are we? Oh man. A leaking water pipe. My hand looks like five ice pops. Look at sleeping beauty. Resting as if there was no care in the world. No cold. No warmth. No sense! What an idiot I am to hook up with this guy. No direction whatsoever. Just aimless wandering. Like the wind. Here today. Gone today. No feel. No touch. Neither warm nor cold. Neither loved or love. Neither dead or alive. Just aimless wandering from town to town. From flophouse to flophouse. From pigsty to pigsty. It's getting light. Warming up too. Much better. Gonna tell this schlub that I am hitting the road, Jack. High and by! Hasty Banana! So long, amigo! Hey, friend, wake up. I said wake up! Oh oh! He's assumed room temperature. I knew it was going to dust. You may be right but at least I would feel good for about three seconds. So be it my fine feathered friend. Now please pause your nuisance complaints and let get some rest for tomorrow's adventures. Another night happened. At least I can take control of this situation. Hey, friend. Hello there. I was or should I say, we were waiting for you. You were! Wow! This guy actually had a plan! Glad to meet you. Which hotel are we going to? The hotel name is meaningless. But your travels have ended. Your time in the world of gray, the time of nowhere, the time of the second hand has ceased. Welcome here! Welcome to the Paradise Room.

Curmudgeon

Oh my gods! My tooth! My blasted tooth! Aah! Aah! Where are you wife? You bellowed husband of mine? I was not bellowing but in tremendous pain. Oh, I am sorry O Lord and master. Flattery will get you everywhere. Now. What to do. You are asking me my Lord and you are the head here. That is true my lovely. In this case I cannot function or be myself. Stop all this banter and get Herm. Herm? Yes, Herm! What took you so long to get here? I was working on some new disease for which I have no name for since I don't even know what it does yet. And besides, you ordered me to do that. That is totally contrary to reasons I have you here. Yes. You must carry out your duties as I have prescribed to you. And the chief among them is my health and welfare. But Lord…But nothing! Get over here and make me well. Yes, my Lord. Let's see here. Oh, yes. Oh my my, yes. That bad Herm? Yes. That bad Lady Zee. Well what is it? Tell me or I will make you the lowest of the low and the ugliest of the ugliest. Now out with it you toad! First of all, Zee, calm down. Just a sign of old age and benign neglect. Really now? Yes really my Lord. I don't believe you. I firmly believe that lately the neighbors down the block are causing this. How so? I'll tell you how so. They bring their kind into this area with their ideas and their beliefs. They steal away those that are ours and lessen us but also make us ill and withering. I do not believe that my Lord husband. Neither do I. I say this not only as your doctor but one who has been with you for all the ages. That mumbo jumbo all sounds very good to you. But remember this: without me there is no you. We are keenly aware of that. But there will always be those who follow. Even if there is only one man in each corner of the world will we still exist. If not in a physical sense, but in their heart, mind, and soul. It is this that we should be concerned with: complacency, unconcern, and misguidance by those false and untrue. Your logic is sound and impregnable. Thank you my Lord. You should be thanking me since all your being is of my doing. There it is! There is what? My Lord! You have it! A toothache? I know that you fool! No, no! NO WHAT! Your sense of things is as sharp as ever my Lord Zee! Really? Despite all that is going on? Yes, yes. Despite our immortality, there will be an end. Oh! An end to ignorance. An end to complacency. An end to the deepest swamp. And, yes, an end to us. An end to superstition. An end to all this that surrounds us. We must move aside to let the fresh air of truth and common sense to enter the room. We must allow all men to be free and unloose the shackles of ignorance and false piety. We must allow the true man to live. We must allow him to think! Set aside and move forward toward true knowledge and displace a closed mind with the yearning of the fruits of the tree that was once despised must now be embraced! He must move forward while we move back into the darkness that is in the archive of mans' heart and soul. We must go my Lord Zeus. Hera, will you come with me? Yes my Lord. And Hermes? Yes. I will follow.

Eclipse

Durwood, Is that you? Well, who else would it be! Are you 'sleep? Yes, I am. You are actually talking to my alter ego, Fenwood who exists in the 3rd, 4th and 26th dimensions. Click, click. Moan. Snore. Cough. Ah, yes. Hello and good morning to you my fine spousal partner! Don't be wise! Go back to sleep and let me talk to this Fenwood character. He's much more pleasant and probably better looking too. Alright then! That's enough! What time is it? It's 8:30 and I've got a problem. You've got a problem! So do I and it's you WAKING up to such nonsense. Now leave me alone. You know I didn't finish work till 2! I know that but I have this problem. Can't it wait? Come to think of it it can. So go back to bed and I talk to you later. Or maybe I would be better off with the alter ego fellow of yours Fenwood in the whatever dimension or universe he exists. You're repeating yourself. You're right. I am repeating myself. Actually not. It's MY alter ego. Her name is Sunny. And she never gets angry and says nice things even if she doesn't mean it. So, from the both of us to the both of you sorry Chalie and happy and sweet nothings! Yeah, nothings. Why does she always have to slam the door? I will never understand. Ugh! Ugh! Snore. Snore. Now that few extra hours did help. Only a little. What a sunny day! YES DEAR! Oh hi dear! How was your sleep? Even though you woke me up earlier...I woke you up? No, I didn't. Yes you did. No I didn't. I was not here this morning. I went out to the track and ran a couple laps. And then I did my nails and...Don't try to play it off. Alright already! I forgive you! Forgive me for what? I didn't do anything to you. Like I said, I was out all this morning and only got back a few minutes ago. Okay. Alright. Never mind. How about some coffee? I feel very confused. A cup of Joe is what I could use. Coming right up my honey! Hmm. Hmm. Not here. Not there. Then where? Ugh! Where's my coffee dear? What? I said where is my coffee. I told you 20 minutes ago I need something to straighten myself out. So you want me to hit you in the head with a baseball bat. Or would a five iron be more to your liking. Your luck with these things is poor to say the least. Bashing you in the head would be a step up for these toys. At least they would be used productively. Now, I am really confused! So do you want that coffee or not? NOT! I'm going out. Maybe to run. Maybe to fix myself up. BYE! I must be losing my marbles. One minute nice, the next not so nice. Almost like Jekyll and Hyde. I mean Nurse Jekyll and Miss Hyde. You mean WHO dear? Who? What? Where? Yes, Durwood. Please meet Miss Hyde or should I say Annie Lowe. Annie, Miss Hyde – whatever you want to call me. It is all the same. Or is it Durwood? Ah. Um. Hmm. Oh, by the by, there is one more person I want you to meet. But first, I need you to look at yourself in the mirror. However gruesome it might be for both of us. Two of you? Now that is frightening! See your real self before you start lambasting others. None of us is perfect. Sometimes people have to hold their tongue in dicey situations. We do it because it is not worth the time or effort to squabble about the price of tea in China or the newspaper landing in the trash. Give it up Durwood. I have nothing else to say. Please let me introduce that person I promised you at the beginning of this confession. Please look closer in the mirror. Say hello to Fenwood of the, what was it? I think it was 3rd, 4th, or was it the 26th dimension. It's all in the mirror. IT'S all in you! You are that person! Remember: you make life what it is!

Education

Another trip back from those dull meetings with clients. All I get is, "We don't think your company is right for us." Or, "They are not giving us the support we need. Morality is cheap but what we need is cash." I guess they are right but I have to tow the company line. Looks like I need a little gas. Hey fella, filler up. Let me buy a pack of cancer sticks to hold me over. What? No more left on the card? Wonderful! Even the company card is useless. Here's the cash to cover the rest. Alright. Have a good night. Let me light up. Aah. Much better. Much much better. Let's see. Route 472 South. That's what we want. Looks good. State trooper. Glad this radar works. Let's tootle along here. Nice and quiet. Exactly what I need for this part of the trip, Get home and just fall down on the couch and pass out cold. I am envious already. Corporate already has the information it needs so I don't need to be bothered with them. Hmm. Hmm. La di da. Ho hum. What's this up ahead? Cop car? No. Accident? No. Stalled truck? Maybe I can help. You know what? He's probably got a cell phone anyway. Good. I can just keep rolling. Oh...he's moving. Good. You're kidding me! A school bus? At this hour? Oh wonderful! This guy is straddling both lanes. Any stupid move on my part would cause my will to go in effect. Alright, we'll just deal with this guy until he turns off. It's been about a half hour now. Still going the same way. Let me see here. I know another way. It's longer but I am not making any time here. There it is. Left and here we go. Crappy road but it says home on it. Glad to be away from that bus. Hmm. Hmm. Puff. Puff. Ah! The pause that refreshes. What's this? A tractor trailer! On this road! Man this is just not my day I mean night. I am getting so tired of this. Alright. Not much I can do. Good! He's turning off into the rest stop. Go ahead, rest. Let me get home. Railroad tracks. Now what? Bells and whistles. Whoosh. Whoosh. Man this thing is still going. Hey look! The circus is passing through. Okay. Finally. Thud. Thump. Not much left to go. It looks like another half hour and that's it. End of corporate shilling for another day. Ice Cream Joe's. Look at them. I thought they were all gone. Wow! Loved those sundaes on Tuesdays! Love to have one but it looks like they are closed. Guess I get some out of the fridge when I get back. Don't remember this place. The old Greenfriars Graveyard. Looks spooky. Looks like nobody takes care of it. Desolate. A shambles. People all forgotten. Probably in life too. When I go, it will be the same after a couple of years. The flowers will all wilt. The weeds start to grow. No daisies for me! Ah. Here we are home. At last. My humble abode! The mail, bills, bills, and more bills. Adverts for get rich quick schemes. Trash. Here's a postcard from my kid brother. Enjoying the honeymoon in sunny Aruba. See you in two weeks. Great kid. Great gal he married. I am sure envious. But business is no business for a wife. Maybe I'll give Trish a call for lunch Thursday. Fun girl. Lucky me. This couch sure feels good. On TV? Let's see. Nothing. Nothing. More nothing. Hey! What's this! Old reruns of Super Quack. One of my favorite cartoons. Watched that day and night! What else? Lookie here! "The Battling Truck Circus" is on. Wow. Another great kid show. What is this? A picture of me and my best friend Norville. Where did this come from? It came from my Aunt Jilly. Oh! He passed away last week from some disease I can't even pronounce. I'll send some really nice flowers. I wish I could go but this is on the other side of the country. Really sad. You know. Sitting here I really feel like I have missed the little things in life. Growing up and enjoying life. Cartoons, toy trucks and buses, the circus. Best friends. I suppose there is really nothing wrong with reliving the past to ease out of the dis-comfort of the present. You know…I will go to Norville's farewell. Can't put a price on those intangibles since their value is immeasurable. The little things. The little things…

Epsilon

Misha, what are you doing? Nothing father. Nothing father? Yes nothing father. That is the wrong thing to say. And what should have I said? Do not speak back to your father that way. You are being impertinent. I'm what? I will not repeat myself to a child that will not listen to her father. Father, I am not a child. I am a grown woman who knows exactly what impertinent means and you are the one being that. How about the word obtuse? That's enough Misha! I am not impertinent or this thing you call obtuse. I am YOUR FATHER and that is enough of your big words and disobedience. You are not too old to be punished across your backside, despite your mothers' pleas. God rest your mother. She gave you good looks and a sassy mouth. I had lots of problems with her and now I have problems with you. But she was a great woman and a great mother despite her flaws and bad cooking. Misha, I know you are a good cook and will make a great wife to some young man. You must be respectful and obedient to his every wish. This whether he is with his friends or in his house or his wishes for children. Or even in the most private of all moments. Now, Misha…Father, we are not going to have this discussion again. I thought we settled it. We did settle it, daughter. We will have no discussion. It was not meant for back and fro, but a final word and respectful obedience from my child. Besides, your mother – God rest her soul! – wanted it that way. No she did not! And you this! My daughter Misha! How dare you say this about her! I have known this woman for over thirty years and will know her for all eternity. She plainly stated that on her death bed that this is what she wanted for her loving daughter. Father, father. I must disagree. What! Yes, Father, disagree. But I was there when she pleaded that you carry on this tradition, the dowry, the fruit of your love, and all that is encompassed! No, no, no, Father! You couldn't take it anymore. Like a good husband, you were overcome by grief and had to leave her bedside. But I, not YOU stayed as a good child to the very end. I sobbed, but I sobbed not as much as to her passing but to her wonderful mind! Her freedom from the past was ending and a new reality took over. One of enlightenment and clarity. One of satisfaction and completeness. In a sense, a mental resurrection from old and dingy to new and well-suited. Misha, what are you talking about? You hurt my heart with spears of poison and acid! I cannot endure such talk! You must, Father. You must! Mother said just before you came back in the room, that you made life a living Hades with your stubbornness and intransigence. The worn out and moth-ridden ideas of life and existence. She only said what she said to please you. Even at her final moments, she needed to clear up these things. She backed you one-hundred percent on all your decisions, right, wrong and otherwise. But mother could not leave the shell with all that on her breast. She needed to be free from old notions and hurtful wounds. Yes, she loved you, but only enough to do her duty as wife and mother. Her little piece of heaven existed in some dark corner of her heart. A place where no one was allowed. Even to her husband a place that was sacrosanct. All this came to me at the very end. She needed to make her only place of heaven on earth exist. If not for one minute at least her final breath. For mother, that one nuance of time was just enough to find peace. Remember, Father, we each make our very piece of earth as what we make it. Whether it be scorched and soiled or preened and smooth. It is ours and no one can take it away. So, Father, is THAT the wrong thing to say now? No, my precious one, no.

Finale

I need to get some sleep. Man, I just hurt all over. Those office parties are something else. Or was it the bookkeeper's birthday? She did look funny with the water cooler jug over her head! And she sure knows how to juggle those numbers! Yeah. Huh. Hmm hmm. Alright, that's enough. To the pillow I go. Wait a minute! Am I even home? I don't even recognize this place. I do have my cell. I hope there's a charge to it. Not much. I don't even have a signal. Just great. Screw it. You know I don't even have the strength to move. So be it! Here I stay. What's this then? Hello. Is this Gerald Mcbane? No, it is not. Now…Are really sure? I got this number from his brother and…Whoa! Whoa! Aren't you listening buddy? I said I am not this whoever you said. Now get off my phone! Bye! What a jerk off! Now, to present problems. I forgot. Oh, yes. Where am I? Ouch! Hmm. This and that again. What's this? Another phone call? A waste of my battery! Who is it? Unidentified? Yes hello? May I speak to Gerald Mcbane? What did I just tell you! I am not this Mcvain fellow! You mean Mcbane! Well, whoever you said. Scram before I call the cops! Bye! I'm already annoyed but now I am really angry. Wrong number. Wrong place. Wrong time. Wrong everything! I am in deep mud! Maybe I'll never get out of this place. Now, I am really depressed! Nowhere to turn. Nothing I can do! Must be patient. Yes. That's it. Be patient. For what? I have no control over anything right now. Like a child lost in a crowd. What now? That phone! Didn't I just tell you I am not the Mc whoever fellow. Hey bud…Maybe I would rather talk to you. My name is…I am not concerned what your name is because I am not going to speak to you! I am depressed and alone and don't know what in the world is going on! I can't even think straight, I think! Nowhere to turn! Nowhere to go! Like a lost little lamb. Funny you should day lamb. I think I have the right person on this phone. Since Gerald Mcbane can't be found, I will speak to you I instead. What if I don't want to speak to you? From what I can tell you have no choice. You're disconnected from all things right now. From life. From your friends. If they can be called your friends.

They really don't like you. You're put up with. You have a place to live or should I say exist. You get up. You go to work. You come home. You have an "adult beverage". You pass out. And the next day begins. And it ends. And it goes on and on and on. Sam cycle. Same ol' vicious cycle. A straight line with no end. A square with no beginning. Bumping into one wall and continuing on to the next. And so on and so on. Yes. You are the Gerald Mcbane I am looking for. YOU all are Gerald Mcbane. YOU all are Susie Withers. YOU all are. No plan. No direction. No nothing! Just dark empty shadows. Just empty shells of existence that start at birth and end at six feet under. Yes. The only thing that has a beginning and end is life itself. That you have no control over. However, the rest is yours. Fill it with life and abundance and not smoke and mirrors. Fill it with fruit and daisies and cats and dogs and things that can't be touched but can only be realized and that is life. That is life in a nutshell. You can garnish life with a sprinkle of this and a touch of that. But that is what life is all about. Just have the basics and the rest is yours. The rest is yours. Oh by the way, your battery is just about gone. Remember. Remember. Remem…Re…Oh man! Oh man! Yes. Yes! Ye…Thomas, this truth is not ever easily accepted. You should know this well. I throughout the ages realized this. Yes, Gabriel, throughout the ages. The agnostics are always difficult but at least the atheists are either black and white. Let's see. Just one more. Has it been that long. Yes, that long. The final time is here. You know who is next, Thomas. Yes, I do. All I can suggest to you, Thomas, is bring a large supply of burn ointment.

Gnostics

William the 103rd thousand please come hither. Yes my Lord I am here. Oh, I am sorry. I keep forgetting. In this realm, that is a very bad trait to have. Now William, we have decided to give you a chance of redemption. You are more than generous my Lord for giving me another opportunity for...Yes, yes – I know. Many a chance you have been given but we know your heart and soul. It is a simple, yet, well, even if we don't know or if we did, could we even describe it. An uncluttered and tidy existence that manifests itself in an all but one way – the indescribable. Enough of your self – vanity heaped upon a being such as you, William, is not a positive thing. My Lord, I am a humble servant of the wise and wiser. I am not fit to judge myself due to my needed humility and the choice of my missions would be poor to say the least. My soul, you never cease to amaze me at your genuine incorruptibility. Now, for your chapter. You will attend to 4019675-B. You will, as usual, make the needed adjustments and immerse yourself totally for a time yet to be determined. There is a twist or should I say special circumstance that is known only but not to you. Even this circumstance may change while on the road to finality. AGAIN I say AGAIN! Exist as normal and consider none of the other things I have told you! You have been chosen and you will do as I say. Yes my Lord. I will do the very task you have given me. If I fail – William you will not fail and if by chance you should, the results will be most disastrous and a fate that is darker than dark. Be on your way, William the 103rd thousand! You know, Steven, this is not as severe as you make it out to be. I know Augustus. But William must be imprinted with that concept of self-importance and not be as simple as he makes himself out to be. He is a very integral cog in this wheel and that he must not know. If everything goes as planned, he will never know. I never understood your soul Steven. Even with all of your being, Augustus? Ha, my Lord Steven, ha my Lord! Steven, I am sensing. Myself as well Augustus. It is still quite remote and far away, but still recognized. Yes, Steven, yes. It is growing stronger and more toward the apex of time. This is incredible!

Incredible for the outcome? No, the outcome as we have thought is not surprising but the stuff of matter is! I do not follow, my Lord Steven. That is why you are not entrusted with any tasks that great my Lord Augustus. Your knowledge and wise brow are your saving graces. Aside, the time is nigh! It is here! Let us receive this gift with joy and reverence! It is done! William has done his job well. He can now be part of a greater universality that is reserved for a higher race. My Lord Steven! You seem to be drunk with delirious thoughts. No! No! Don't you understand? It is as simple as the soldier who we sent to do our bidding. Each being has a certain knowledge – as unique to them as the stars are in the sky. All beings are important regardless of what this knowledge is. If a person can knit a piece of clothing a certain way and no one else can, the world can be better off, especially if one is cold. If a being can invent a cure for some illness that only one has, his contribution was 100% and complete. And remember, my Lord Augustus, if someone can just smile in a certain way and remove a burden from another, that too, is 100%. Not all knowledge comes from a book or higher realm. It can come from the soul or whatever you wish to call it. Remember Augustus, we are not the guardians of that knowledge – that comes from the heart and mind of the individual. We make sure that all beings are incorporated with goodness and self-worth and no being is more superior to another. One of our more receptive and simpler hearts said, "All men are created equal with certain inalienable God given rights…" I, to this time, Steven, still shudder at the strong impulse when these words flow through me. I too, Augustus. I too.

Guest

You're a stranger in this here town. Good observation barkeep. I would like a sarsaparilla with a dash of lemon. A what with a what did you say mister? A sophisticated and modern barkeeper such as yourself who tends to this fine – hmph – class of gentlemen and cowpokes should know about what a sarsaparilla is. Or is the part that unnerves you is the lemon part? If so, substitute a pinch of honey…You know what honey is? I'm afraid I reckon so. She is at home tending the little unes. No you oaf! Honey! Like the bees! Oh yeah mista'. I know all 'bout the bees. It was just right yestaday that ole' Pa Perkins got hisself stung by some twunty or thurty bees when he tipped over his fishin' line into a hive and woo! Did he ever ran screamin' and hoopin' and hollerin' until he fell into ole' Lake Hobo! Now what was it you wanted? Oh, never mind! Just a demitasse of coffee, black with exactly two sugars. Sir, I run a 'spectable place here. No cussin' here! I make even the toughest hombres and cowpokes restrain thesselves from foul language! Hmm. I give up on this conversation. Let me ask you this: What is it that I can drink in here that you can understand and won't have to give me a very long and very wide story? Well why didn't you say so! I gots somethin' here that's mos' popular with the finer gentlemen and most respectable ladies. As a matter of fact, Mrs. Winthrop, who runs a…well let's say, a boardin' school for young ladies who are workin' their way thru medical school, commented to me about the finer aspects of this little drink. Really now Dr. Barkeep! Yep! Yep! Yep! I invented it myself with a little help from my ole' 'cus Wendell from down yonder the hills over just south of town. But I couldn't have done it without the town's primary medical physician and hangman when the judge comes 'roun Dr. Archibald U. Sweetwater. He delivered all my youngins' and only charged me a nickel each and only eight cents for the twins. He is a regular all 'roun guy! Well, I suppose I could try this rather innocuous looking concoction. How much will this delicacy of the house set me back? Mista, I taken a good likin' to you so here is what I do for you. If you like it, pay me what you think its worth. As a matter of fact, I think you'll like it so much that I'll let you have it for nothin'. Nothing? Nothin! Hmm. Well let me try this. Should I stand up and drink or should I sit down? Perhaps you should lie down on the couch in the corner after you take a slug. Okay. I do feel somewhat tired from all this excitement. Well, here we go. Um. Very tasty indeed. My my! Wonderful aroma. Such a sweet aftertaste. What did you say you called it? I never did tell ya' the name. It is called "The Bitter End". But it is sweet. It more has to do with the end and not the beginning. What? You see Mr. McDermott that…How did you know my name? You see Mr. Mcdermott we know all about you or people just like you. We live a simple life here. Nothing fancy. Nothing gaudy. Nothing beyond two or three syllables in a word. Mom's apple pie. Aunt Betty's sewing club. The volunteer fire department. Cousin Billy neckin' with his girl out on Frog's Pond. And so on and so forth. A life that is viable. A life that is simple. Get away from modern contraptions and do-hickeys and thingamabobs. Yes, they are inevitable but not here. People surround themselves with the basic pleasures of life. When they are ready, they accept these things as all must do. But, it must be in their time and in their way. They will sort out the junk from needs. They will make use of these things as they see fit. It will be in their good time. Oh, by the way, remember the doctor I told you about? Oooom. Ooh. Aagh. I will accept that as a yes. Dr. Sweetwater's middle initial is "U", which stands for undertaker.

Headache

Oh man, everything hurts. I have a splitting headache. My back feels like it is split in two. My legs – it almost like I can't feel them – but I know they are there. Just everything. Wait a minute! This mattress feels really firm. Maybe it is because everything is all screwed up, I don't know. Oh, I know what happened. I went out last night to the club to hang out with the guys and see who we could pick up. It either went really well and I am in some chick's house or I am lying in the gutter on Fifth and Western. What a mess! Today must be Wednesday or was it yesterday? Oh boy. Boss man is going to be really annoyed with me. Today was the day I was supposed to meet with the firm of Williams, Williams and Boozer and aah. That hurts and this hurts and everything hurts. Oh God this pain is unbearable. This is the last time I mix drinks with those pills. Those pills…oh those pills! I wish I could get my hands on some of those! I would still be aching but I would certainly have a smile on my face? Okay. Phase Two! Where am I? How do I get out of here? Uh…oh man…uh…aggh! Regroup. Think clear, maybe. Block out the pain. Let's get ourself together, get up, get out, get dressed and be on our way. Let's see. Open our eyes – if we can – and survey the damage. Ready – one, two, three – here we go. NOTHING! NOTHING? NOTHING! OH CRAP ! Now I am blind. Wonderful. Wait a sec…I had heard the expression blind drunk. Yeah. That must be it. I am so out of it that I literally am blind drunk. Yeah that's it. Okay. Alright. Touch…touch. I can still feel. What have we got here? A tube. Yep. That's it. It must be some kind of feeding tube or blood transfusion. Wow! That's great! I am in the hospital and they are trying to put me back together just like Humpty Dumpty! Talk about scrambled eggs! Reminds me of that chick last week – was Barbara or Denise – I can't tell the difference sometimes. It feels such an assembly line – but oh they are so sweet! But that was last week, this is this week and this is now. Wait a minute! I hear movement or do I feel it? Can't quite tell since I am all screwed up. OUCH! That hurts even more. I think somebody just took that damn tube out. Uh! I – wait a minute. I feel I am being lifted up or moved or something. Can't quite make it out. Now I am somewhere else. THIS IS DARK! Now I don't sense anything. And this is no mattress! OH GOD! WAIT! I hear voices. Can't quite make it out.! Now I am REALLY SCARED! Shh! Be Quiet! What was that? Here we go. "Basement…the room…morgue…autopsy." Then there was no more.

Hesti

You, sir. Come here. Yes. What is your name? Izan is my name. Izan, does your name have a meaning? No sir. It is a traditional name that may have its origins long ago. That is indeed interesting, but no meaning? No tradition? You belong to a shallow history. Indeed I do. We have existed throughout the ages, but no lore exists. A sad thing for today. Is it a thing to dwell on? I cannot. But why this discussion on my name? Perhaps a more important discussion should follow. Concerning what, Izan? It is you who beckoned me. That is correct, but that discussion has already happened! Yes? Yes! By your very words you have demonstrated that you are unconcerned and as dimensional as a scroll of wheat. Flat. A flounder with two legs. No depth. No meaning. Only concerned with the here and now not the then and there or the will be and place. That is why you are who you are. No past. Ignorance with haste and the undeep. All your past is gone. You throw it away for the present. And YOUR name, sir? Infinitum.

Igloo

Mr. Wackenhutt, please report to the principal's office. Mr. Wackenhutt...Oh you're here already? Miss Somers, I had a feeling you would wish to talk to me. And do you know about what? I seemed to have guessed wrong in the past so I won't speculate now. How smart of you! Miss Somers...Don't Miss Somers me! The amount of calls and letters about you has become unmanageable and entirely inappropriate. Even the commissioner has made an issue of this. You mean your brother the commissioner? That's enough, Mr. Wackenhutt! I am entirely annoyed by your complete and utter insolence! But what I don't understand why you are still here! With all the people against you and ready to feed you to the sharks, there is somebody or something or shielding your scrawny hide from complete and utter oblivion. You were recommended by these patrons of yours and you are as hard to pry loose as a rotten board. Now, Mr. Wackenhutt, we can be reasonable...Miss Somers, you mean your brother can be reasonable...Mr....Please enough of the extraneous and just between you and me. Okay? I am listening. Good. That's a start. Now, Mr. Wackenhutt, you have been here two years. One as an assistant and the balance as primary. And in all that time as assistant, you were a good little helper who did his work and did what was told. As soon as we moved you to your present position, all kinds of bad stuff has broken out. Miss Somers, that is your view. Not just mine, Mr. Wackenhutt, but a majority if not all of the board members. At first, we merely re-instructed you on proper procedure as stated in the manuals. As time wore on, you were suspended for a day here to a day there. That seemed to have no effect on you and you continued to be in violation. More letters and more days. More this and more that. And on and on and on. I believe or should I say the board believes that you should be dismissed out of hand immediately if not sooner. Amazingly enough, we have not heard from your guardian angel or angels so it looks like you have been let out to dry, Mr. Wackenhutt. So, please retrieve your things and you have till noon to vacate this building or I shall have you forcibly removed by the police.

Is that understood? Yes, completely, Miss Somers. However...However nothing Mr. Wackenhutt. Get your things and leave and don't let the door hit your backside. Miss Somers, may I speak freely since I am no longer in your employ? You may but just briefly. Fair enough. I came to this miserable little institution two years ago with a few dollars and many ideas. Today, I have still less dollars and many more ideas. You see, ideas are cheap – practically nothing. Worthless bits of atoms and neurons mixing together like a stew or a salad. The croutons are always good, but in this case, stones and pebbles are inedible. You and your like are these bits of dinosaurs that became extinct millions and millions of years ago. Cold, sharp, and without feeling you added yourselves to our meals. Maybe not just you, but people like you throughout the ages. From the first primordial slop that coagulated on the shore to the ignorance and superstitions that existed through the dark ages to the Inquisition to the witch burnings at Salem. I can go on and on but choose not to so as not to demean my message. Yes, Miss Somers and your brother the commissioner, there is something and not someone shielding me. It is the enemy of ignorance and erudite thinking. It is the right to think. It is bearing of the truth from the soul. It is the freedom to believe in one's own destiny and not to be controlled so as to fit in a compartment that is neat, tidy, and generically the same as its neighbor. The right to be different. No, Miss Somers, it is you who are fading away. It is you who are now growing small and shriveled. It is you who must leave by noon.

Imperialis

Good morning, M'lord. Good morning jokester. Did Your Majesty sleep well? Not at all Roth. Not at all. Pray tell what was bothering you Sire? Unfortunately, the weight of the world and things generally those of your station in life cannot understand. My Lord, you are so right! It is constantly amazing to myself and those of my caste that we can function at all! It is only with the guidance of persons of your stature and kindness that we can accomplish even the most menial tasks. Roth, you speak only the truth. I cannot deny the lowliness of the people in your level. However, dear funny-man you are somewhat different, somewhat smarter and somewhat shrewder than most of your class. My Lord! How do you flatter me! It is true that I am somewhat more civilized than most of my people. However, none of this would be the case if not for your personal and unselfish devotion in the maturing and shaping of my crude manners and lowly intelligence. You do have a point, Roth. However, we must talk about the things at hand. Shall I leave Lord so that you may discuss these heavy worldly matters with those who you call your advisers? Absolutely not. I wish to talk these things with you, dear joke-maker. Me? Yes, you. But I...But nothing! I command you to give me counsel or I will send you back to the fields so you can toil from sunrise to sunset. If you insist, my Lord. I insist now open your mind and I will stretch your puny little brain to great lengths so that you can rise up and show the people that wisdom and knowledge is as powerful as the sword. Yes, M' Lord. I will listen. I told you before that I could not sleep. The fate of this country is in the hands of a small band of brigands with a maniacal leader. He has escaped our clutches for years now. Every time we capture one of his legion, the poor fellow always commits suicide before we can persuade to tell us more. His last words are always the same as others. My Lord? The word is...I cannot be strong enough to say it. It is...It is...Fiat lux. Do you know what that means, Roth? I am too stupid my Lord to comprehend such words. It sounds and this is strictly a guess, some ancient and dead language? After much research and discussions with our scholars, they are unable to come up with any guess. But I suspect dear funnyman that your guess can be as good, but not better than all the wisdom in this palace. You are right, Your Majesty in that thinking. I sense something more sinister, Roth. I can tell by your hooked nose. It is starting to twitch. A mere itch, Sire. Hmm. Roth, I happened to know that before you came here, your background was examined. A simple life with simple uneducated people. YOU are smarter than them? I mean, as a simpleton with simpleton people. Roth, your time is up! Your identity has been known for some time now. You have been under close scrutiny by those loyal to me. True patriots. True members of this kingdom. King or should I say, incompetent. You are an idiot. You are a simpleton yourself. You were the illegitimate son of a wash woman who was forced into submission by a drunken member of the upper class. Real smart of the Lord Fennel! You are but a plant! Your mind is an asparagus. Your hair are corn weeds. Your eyes are of olives – black and empty! Your heart! Oh your heart! It is a mushroom. A poisonous slab of brown fungus that is great food to the swine. These swine do not slop in mud but the halls of your palace and on an occasion, into the bed of your mistress. She is just a vulture. Feeding off of your naivete and insecurities she plans and plunders your very soul of sawdust and rancid fish. You have no feeling. You have no heart. You know nothing that surrounds you. You are fed lies by your advisers. You are told that you are beloved. You are told that you are divine. This just like the Roman Emperors. I suspect they do this out of fear of livelihood and their own mortality. You sir, are nothing! Just fluff and emptiness. A bag of feathers. No substance. No nothing! MY LORD! FIAT LUX! Roth you pig! You are right to say that. Those will be your last words. No, you trash. Your last words will be FIAT TENEBRAE!

J'accuse

This is a very heavy thing that is borne. Yes, my friend, very heavy. A person's whole being is at stake. I must be precise, accurate, and have no doubt whatsoever in my mind. Unfortunately the facts that I have at my disposal are flimsy. There is the hearsay. There is the innuendo. There is all of this and all of that. My mind is awash with all these things. Yes, friend. It is a burden that I wish not for my deepest enemies. I understand your mind. That is why you were selected for this onerous task. There must have been better. I suppose so. However, you were chosen regardless of all these things. We are not unaware of your shortcomings. We are looking for a simple balance of right and right, not an extraordinary IQ. You flatter me too much. You did accept this challenge of a maze. You know from the deepest fathoms of your inner being that you can decide this thing. Or at least decide on an indecision which can still preserve a man's fate. Thank you again friend. To the facts or to these words that may seem as facts. Yes, many to look at and many to challenge. Yes, my friend, many. We have person A saying that this is the man who did these horrible things. It is very detailed in its details.

These occurred over many years and were conducted in the person's residence. Why would this person go to the residence if he knew what would happen? Supposedly, person A was enticed by the suggestion that he was a father figure and needed to be secure in some way. That makes sense. It continued until person A became of age and moved to another locale. I see. This other person, Person B would encounter on trips out no other places. This also, throughout the years. There are many examples of this and so on and so forth. It has now come to our attention from information gathered that the accused has been living a low-key life in the southern part and has made no attempt to disguise or shield himself from view. This is very odd for a person who has done so many bad things. Friend, perhaps the best way of handling things is through plain sight. He may say, "I am here," or, "I have nothing to hide." Or we may just have the wrong person. There are people with similar backgrounds, names, statures. We can truly make such assumptions that are wrong and deadly to a man's presence. And this appears to be the situation. To assume that this person is guilty of such awful things makes the accuser just as complicit. "Oh, it looks just like him. Therefore in my view, it is." Then, we have the busybodies who take whatever they can find and ruin a man's life because it is entertaining. They do not realize the harm that is done. That is why it is so important to be correct in our assertions. It is true that the accusations are real and very much happened. However, the problem we have here is of identification. As I have said before, there are similarities and there are not. I am not willing to forsake a man's life so it can make for a coffee table book or tabloid magazine or even a shocking revelation on the worldwide stage. No, friend, no. If the man is not willing to come forward and defend his innocence, there is nothing we can do and cannot assume from his silence that he is indeed the party in question. He may not even know what he is accused of. All he should say that he is not that monster and to leave him alone before his entire being is ruined. A man has only himself and reputation. On a higher level, God. We may never know and it may not be in the scheme of things for us to know. Therefore, I am. And you are you. And that is all we know for sure.

Legacy

On behalf of all the shareholders...On behalf of all our customers...On behalf of all your co-workers...I would like to extend our deepest appreciation for your many years of service for this company. I know I would be remiss if I did not include a special mention from myself. Larry, you have been one of the most genial and generous chairmen I have ever had the pleasure to know and work for. From the first day I met you in the shifting department when we were both rookies. To the times we each mirrored each other's climb up the ladder to where we are today. The finest gentleman I have ever had the pleasure of knowing...Let me introduce to you Mr. Larry Deuce – retiree extollent! Thank your George for those kind words. Let me say I cannot add much more to what was just said. Words won't properly convey my innermost thoughts and feelings I have right now. I have been waiting 42 years for this permanent vacation. Fishing, fishing, and more fishing is what I plan to do. But, now to much more serious matters. There has been much talk at the water cooler and at the snack bar as to who I will recommend to the board of directors as my successor. Some say Thommy Gann. Some even more say George. Some of who will remain known only to me. I have given much thought and will suggest to the board Mr. Roger Billingsworth. Now, now. Hush! I say hush! This is not a popularity contest nor an election. It is my call and that is it. If those of you who disagree with me, you may call in your proxy and put forward a name. Whether it be anybody I mentioned or somebody from left field, that is your privilege and right. But as far as I am concerned, Billingsworth is my man. Thank you and have a good night. George, I am so sorry to hear that. It's all right, Bobby. Down deep I suspected that Deucey was a hypocrite and liar. From day one I suspected these qualities were his only ones. Whatcha gonna do? Go home and cry? No...Not me...I will continue here in the trenches, be a good soldier, etc., etc. Good night Bobby and thank you for your shoulder. No problem Georgie. Where is this elevator? Here I am all retired and can't even get out to my car! It seems like something is trying to keep me here. Oh well, another five or ten minutes after 42 years won't make much difference. Here it is. Oh hello, George. Good evening Mr. Deucey. Why all this formality? You see, you are a former work colleague and are not entitled to call me by the familiar. Therefore, it is Mr. Thomas. So be it Mr. Thomas! I thought you were a better person than to humiliate me in front of a large audience. At least you could have told me in private and saved me from losing face. Even though we were friends this is how you treat me. I can get over not being your successor but the rest is the rest. That is the way it goes, Mr. Thomas. You were a good colleague and good friend but you were not up to the task I chose Billingworth for. He has great business acumen and is very shrewd and…Nephew? Go ahead Mr. Deucey. Say it! SAY IT! Your nephew. Yes, my nephew. So what is it to you? Right now, nothing, Shortly, everything. You see Mr. Deucey, the audience that you were standing in front of were not your employees. What! That is right. Since you never bothered to come down from your ivory tower you had absolutely no idea what the people who work for you look like. So who were all those people? For years, each employee has contributed a small amount to a fund so we could hire folks to come and be with you on your getaway. You see, Mr. Deucey, these loyal folks who worked for you couldn't stomach you for at least 20 minutes. And neither could my father. Your what! Yes, my father. He knew from the get go that you were a complete fraud and backstabber. So, being my father's son and a son who could pass as him, I went in his stead. I could not stand to see my father treated as garbage when he was your most trusted friend and employee. Remember, Mr. Deucey, what goes around comes around. And we have gone full circle.

Nereids

Good morning Mr. Phelps. Good morning to you, Dr. Smith. And how have you been since our last visit? I am assuming you are okay since you only called me five times instead of the usual ten. I do apologize for my many interruptions, especially the ones at 3 am in the morning. Remember, that was my last goal not to call you so many times. That is true Mr. Phelps. And I feel that is a vast improvement since we started six months ago when two or three calls a day were the norm. So, be proud of yourself for the marked improvement and I feel confident that my phone won't be ringing at all different hours. Dr. Smith, I appreciate your humor and thank you very much for all that you have done to this point. Of course, Mr. Phelps. Also, have you been taking that special supplement I gave you last week? It is completely herbal in form and non-habit forming. And from what I understand from other patients, not bad in taste, either. You're right Doc. It has a pleasant minty taste with a tinge of fish flavor. Not bad with goulash either. That's what I like to hear, Mr. Phelps. That is what I like to hear! Now, to business. So tell me how you have been coping since our last chat? Well doctor it's been like this…I have been having these weird sensations of late. Really? Please go on Mr. Smith. And I can't be sure when and where they happen. Sometimes they happen at night I think. But mostly during the day – yes, during the day and sometimes when I go to the market or work. Please go on. I feel as though I am being followed by a group of people or just being watched by just one or two. Very interesting Mr. Smith. Very interesting! Continue. And I can't be sure but I think they are all women – itself not a bad thing but I never considered myself to be more than an average looking guy. Mr. Smith, that is also part of my therapy to help you build self-esteem and confidence in all aspects of life, from the minutiae to the grand. So, pardon my interruption and continue on Mr. Smith. They frightened me at first, but as the days wore on, I became sad that I wouldn't see them anymore, but then, one by one or group by group they started to appear, so felt very good and quite comfortable. And on your way over, did you notice these women companions? Not as many but nonetheless they were there. Like I said, only about two or three. And you felt good? Yes, I did and yes, I do! We have made genuine progress Mr. Smith or should I say you have made genuine progress toward a well-being that is on par with the rest of society. So, this is what I want you to do Mr. Smith – take the supplement I have given you every other day instead of every day. And our next appointment shall be in three weeks instead of two. Can you work with that Mr. Smith? That will be fine Doctor and we will see you then. And may I still call you if necessary, Dr. Smith? Yes, you may always do that. Now, I shall see you then and have a good evening. You too, Doctor. Well, Mr. Phelps, good to see you this morning. You look like a brand-new person! You look like a man with self-confidence and with a certain bravado that is reserved for the upper-crust of society. Have you won a million dollars in the lottery or a trip to Hawaii? I wish Doctor, I wish. I don't know what you put in that concoction of yours but it sure did work! No, Mr. Phelps. The only concoction that worked were the ingredients in your head! All I did was help rearrange them and put them all in order – like ducks in a row. And the women who followed you – what about them? At first, I didn't see them but for all of one or two and that was quite infrequent. After about a week or a week and a half, there were no more to be seen. And you know what? That was fine. I kind of miss seeing those pretty women but as they say, there are more fish in the sea. So, Mr. Phelps, you sound quite well, high-spirited, and self-confident. And you didn't even call me. Well, Doc, I started to, but I said, why bother the man when he has done so much for me. That is my job to listen to people when they need help, especially at 3 am in the morning. Excellent. So for our next appointment...Nothing personal, Doctor Smith, but don't call us we'll call you! Wow! No offense taken! Mr. Smith, be well and let me know if you need any help in the future. I will. I will. Good day Doctor! Good day Mr. Smith! Not bad for some fish oil and mint herbal tea. Let's see. Ah, yes! Hello, is this Mr. Stansfield? Good morning Mr. Stansfield. This is Dr. Smith again. Your girls did a wonderful job. I would like to retain your agency for future projects. Yes, men as well for when I have female patients. Excellent Mr. Stansfield. Excellent!

Oedipus

Dr. Mares, welcome. Dr. Venice, welcome. Dr. Plute, welcome. As you know, this one patient of ours is extremely sick. As I recall Dr. Bright, a chronic one at that. That is correct, Dr. Venice. Dr. Bright, we appreciate your incredible devotion to this cause, but at what point do we say that enough is enough? Or enough is enough for your tenure as chief? Is that a threat Dr. Plute? Take it for whatever you wish, Dr. Bright. At some point one must say, "This patient is terminal," or, "We cannot cure stubbornness." In my view, that is how each one of you can be described. Stubborn, irresolute, and a host of other maladies that would take ions to refute by your lopsided view of things. Would you like me to take out the "Book of All Things"? Chapter by chapter. Verse by verse. Disease by disease? I thought not. Can you still look at yourselves in the mirror of time and say that is not true? My patience has run thin with all of you and all the colleagues who hide behind you cloaks. Shall I dismiss all of you and seek further those who share the right way of things? See! I have struck a nerve! Who wishes to leave first? Who is indignant more than so the others? Yes, you fools. You and you and you over there. This is a big box we are in and there are many small boxes within. The key is that all are in the same box. But boxes can be weak if not packed correctly. Then they must either be repaired, repacked, or discarded. You and that one and the other one can be repaired but can also be trashed. And as you know, it can be done on a whim or known in advance but no shield can be strong enough. Choose and choose wisely. One's fate is in your hands. If I have to wait more than one nuance all is lost and the patient becomes fatal. Thank you Doctors for your attention. Dr. Bright is correct in his dialogue. A mere threat of mortality is bad enough. That lasts but for one second. Guilt lasts time eternal until a negative fate befalls. That time is unknown. I believe we have become selfish and self-important in the matters of all things. Friends and colleagues, our shame is real and our sin of vanity is exposed on the cliffs. Let it die and its carcass be fed to the vultures. We are but mere cogs in the wheel of all and must look out for each other. This

I have learned at this moment. I say all ye must bear witness to the same. We are all connected. We are all in unison. We affect each other as a wave affects the sand on a beach. We sneeze. You shiver. We cough. You sniffle. We cause trauma. You bleed. We heal. You live. Yes, my brothers, we are all linked in a chain forged from fire in the deepest bowels. And breathe the same air from the highest mountains. Yes, we are connected. Yes, we are universal. Yes, we are all we. Yes, we are all Gaia. Yes, we are all earth.

Ogilivia

You have staved off another uprising. Chief Excelsior. Yes, another one. I do not fully comprehend the reason for all these uprisings. We take care of everybody. We feed them. We clothe them. We nurture them back to health. We provide shelter. We have work for them. It is everything in a nutshell. Even the size of 20 times less of your brain, Councilor. Yes, Chief Excelsior. Yes. I go into the streets. I wave to them. I listen to their problems. I comfort them. I give difficulty to those who live in a way that is not palatable to the common people. I came from the land and so I shall be returned to the land. I will be buried with my ancestors in the ancient ground that they deemed sacred and holy. And you, Chief Councilor? I have nothing to add about the living conditions of the people. You treat them kindly, like a grandfather with his grandchild on his knee. Teaching all that is good and bandaging their scrapes and bruises. Wading into their presence. Letting them touch you and breathing your air and tasting the sweat off your brow and all things that a leader is required of you. The end for me, Chief Excelsior, is known only to those who inherit my vial carcass. I will not be among the living to concern myself with such trivialities. My Chief Excelsior, all I know is that I will be at rest and whose fate will be only known to those in the afterlife and poor, stinking soul. Chief Councilor, your talk is rubbish and incoherent. Do you not wish to be held at high esteem when your day is up? Do you not wish to be known for your giving of wise advice to their leader? Do you not wish to be remembered? No, Chief Excelsior. I am of humble origins whose service to you I was pressed. I have no ancestors sort to speak. I have no family. Just a cleaning woman whose claim to fame was to be at once beautiful. Now she is old and haggard. Spending her final days selling daisies and doing odd chores will be her epitaph. I do not know if she is my real mother or the finder of a lost waif late at night. These things I do not know. Chief Councilor! Why did you not tell me these things? Should you or would you have looked differently at the words I uttered? No, Chief Councilor. I wanted you to look at me no differently than you would look at the masses beyond the gate. But we are friends, Chief Councilor. That is where we part company. Chief Excelsior. Why so? Have I not treated you the same or somewhat better, as those masses? And why is that Chief Excelsior? Punish me. Torture me. Feed me to the swine. It hurts my grieving heart to say what I must say. And that is, Chief Excelsior? Are the words you are to spew out? Are they, "Treat you as my son"? Yes, they are. Painfully, yes. Your mother is that cleaning woman. She is here. In this very edifice. She toils away in the anterooms and hallways always cleaning. Always looking for that speck of dust that she will find until her dying day. It grieves me ever so heavily! You pig! You morsel for toads! You liar and conniver! You earth scum! You never deceived me amongst your bells and flourishes! Your love of the people is clouded over by your shadow of shame. Sewer trash! I only stayed in order that I might seek some sort of personal revenge or moral victory. I knew who that woman was. You never adequately bribed those who shielded her. There is no honor amongst thieves. You were given up at a small price. The price of a loaf of bread and a handful of potatoes. Better than the week-old porridge which you thought was very good at the time. I spit on you in life and burn the very ground which will cover you up when the vultures are done with you. I fear that these black winged naysayers will not even have you. The advice I gave you was advice of lies and deceit in order that the hoards may have your neck. And even now they pummel the door. Any last words, CHIEF FATHER? No, my CHIEF SON!

Pearltree

The wisdom no longer exists, Xistus. I know, M' Lord Vergil. A sad day for all things under the sun. The moon as well, Xistus. You speak as a child of the night. All belongs to this earth, whether the noon day rays or the face of the white light. Indeed, Vergil. I cry that even we shall see a seed of thought or a cell of light. Xistus, I have many sorrows as well, but if we have that wisdom, we must scream it from the highest mountain or the…the…bottom of the deepest well. Aye, M' Lord Vergil. As the salmon run upstream and against the tide, we too must wade against the horror of bear and beast. But in the end, a new generation is spawned and a cycle begins anew. You speak as an optimist, Xistus. I must and you must for as the first tree grew, we too, must plant saplings. For fertilizer, the vanity of ignorance and the unchaste of the soul may be used. MAY BE, Xistus? I say MUST BE! Mirrors for the swine!

Piltdown

Wilbur N. Wilson, please come forward. I am here, my Leader. Wilbur N. Wilson you have been selected for this thing. I am aware of this thing and am prepared to carry it out. Good. You in all reality have no choice but I know of your confidence and zeal and for these reasons you have been chosen. Again, most gracious of you, my Leader. Now for the details. I have received into my mind and am ready. There is much to this and for that reason I will put it to you: Are you enough of yourself to carry this out? I shed not a second in contemplating the answer. Wilbur N. Wilson, I put it to you again: Is this a capable thing for your being? I shed not a millisecond in its thinking. Once more I will hurl this storm at you, Wilbur. N. Wilson: Yes or no? I will have my shield and strength to accept bricks and cyclones. You have answered well, Wilbur N. Wilson. My Leader, why do you persist in these inquiries? You have known my heart and soul and yet you persist. Wilbur N. Wilson, it is in my purview to do such. I may know your heart and soul, but I may not know you one instant of time before the final moment. I grieve, Wilbur. N. Wilson, at your mind's wanderings and wonderings. I am much sad at this moment. However, we are logical beings and on that level I can enjoy the fruits of this intercourse. Therefore, Wilbur N. Wilson, be on your way and seek only the truth and question not the wise and good but the ignorant and corrupt. Fear not the insults and blades of falsehoods but challenge them with thoughtfulness and shields of logicalness. Attack them who are unclean with purity and lye. Use that is all good and golden to destroy the evil that lurks in every dark corner and crevice. Fear not with the staff of authority and respect by using it as a weapon to subvert and to create submissiveness to the will of goodness and kindness. Can you do this, Wilbur N. Wilson? I feel ashamed at my questioning. My ignorance is complete. I must re-answer to you my Leader. You will not answer or re-answer or re-re-answer Wilbur N. Wilson. Always your first answer is the most truthful and honest throughout. Wilbur N. Wilson, it is time. "Man was created in the image..."

Polyphemus

Gerald, what is the matter with you? I don't know what is going on! Please help me! Alright, alright. That's what we're here for. So please STAY STILL and sit down on the couch over here. Or if you don't want to sit down, lie down or something down. But please relax or we are forced to do what we usually do. So PLEEEASE sit down. Okay. Alright. I'll do it. But you guys got to help me better this time. No, Gerald. It is we who have to get this thing resolved not just everybody but you. We have had this conversation one-hundred times and this makes one-hundred one. This is it. No more. Finito. End. The last hurrah. Done! Do you understand Gerald? I do. I do. Thank you. I feel better. Let's get on with it. Okay, Gerald. Okay. Now, Gerald, lie down, loosen your cuffs, close your eyes and think of nothing. Clear your mind. Breathe very normally. But, we are going to try something just a little different this time. Good. I see that you are in a stage one frame of mind and soul. Your body will soon achieve that same level. Just a minute…just a minute…almost there. There it is! Okay. Your whole self is now on the same plane of existence – body, soul, mind. That is the perfect conjunction of you, Gerald. The perfect conjunction. Now, let me see. Where are you at Gerald? Or is it, where are all of you at? We are here Dr. Newsome. Where is here? In your presence. In this sphere. In this dimension. In this time. Welcome, members of the universal family. Dr. Newsome, we have met before. Yes we have. Yes we have. It has been a long time. Members of Gerald's body, and all within him, I again bid a complete welcome to the place of inner dissension of the being we call Gerald. Yes, we know it is a sick place. A tormented place. A place that is torn between reality and nothingness. A place that is neither here nor there. But, nonetheless, a place indeed. We must do something different this time. A new way to cleanse Gerald of these phobias and anxieties. A new…Dr. Newsome, we know this already. As a matter of fact, we have known this for some time now. But it has been out of deference to you, Dr., that we have held back. This is out of a great respect we have for you, not only us but of the dimension we come from. Now, I don't feel so bad. I can only say I am extremely honored to be held in such high esteem. I don't know why, but why me? There are others in my profession that are equally capable and probably more qualified than I at what I do. That is true, Dr. Newsome. But we have detected something that is lurking deep in your subconscious that one day, when matured, will be a high holy day for all living things. So, please Dr., accept what we say and be patient at your work. It is done well and done patiently. Ask no more about this and let us tend to the present. Uh, uh, okay! To Gerald! To Gerald. Gerald, wake up Gerald. Gerald? I say wake up. I say be present. I say you are alive! I say you are free! I say take off that eye patch of myopicness! Look at the world around! Realize that your problems, anxieties, fears and other phobias are no less nor no more than others! We are all special in our talents but no different in our fears! Wake up, I say. Wake up and live! Wake up and be free! Wake up and be you!

Purgatory

I am dead. I am alive. I am in a coma. I am wide awake. It is black. It is white. I can't see. I can see for miles. My mind is jumbled. My mind is clear. I am all these things. I am none of these things. I am sad beyond belief. I am joyous beyond reason. I see so many ugly people. I can only see the beautiful people. Where am I? I know exactly my place. Is the west in front of me? Is south barking at my heels? My senses are dulled. I am keen and sharp. I am all these things. I am none of these things. See! I have repeated myself! No! I make a point! A circle is square. A rectangle is four-sided. E does not equal MC squared. Pi does equal three point one four. The sun revolves around the earth. The moon revolves around the earth. I feel stupid. I am a rocket scientist. The summer is cold and bleak. The spring is warm and fresh. What hath been made by God is all wrong. Man can do no right. We are none of these things. People are all these nasties. See! Again I am none of this tripe! I believe all is possible. The daily life we call existence is muddled and corrupted. Our day is perfect and orderly. Any given period of time can be anything. We toil in a perfect world. We are scared of our own shadow. We do not fear the bump in the night. We let our mind become mush. We fill our brain with knowledge. We take the punches. We react. We turn the other cheek. We become resolute. We are in a fantasy world. We grasp reality. We cry. We cheer. We die. We die. Die. Die. Die. There is no other. Yes! There is! A gray, bleak world of existence. We wake up dark and dreary. We go the day dark and dreary. We suffer the slings, the arrows of dark and dreary. There is no middle. There is no beginning. It is a constant iteration of the same. No orange. No green. No yellow. No light hues. Only dark colors. A rainbow of black and white. However, there is no pot of gold at the end. Just broken eggshells and glass. I am dead. I am alive. I…

Midway

Hey Milton. Long time no see! Hi Fred. Haven't seen you…well a millennium. At least. Oh, I did catch a glance as you were working on the elevator. Come to think of it. I thought I sensed a friendly thought. Ever since we downsized, our job classification has grown in contrast to our down time. So much for progress. Yeah, Milton. Well, anything unusual that I should concern myself about? No. Just the usual stuff. I have noticed an uptick in business of late. Too much indecision from all sides. I think you should be careful what you say. I don't think so. We're just a conduit, a way station sort to speak. This is our job. We don't pass judgment. We don't point to that one or this one. Like good soldiers we follow orders. It makes for a sedate and quiet existence, especially for what we do. I guess you are right. See you at the water cooler! Okay, Milty. Let's see the turnover. Hmm. Hmm. Yep. Ah. Let me get myself comfortable. Hey you, come over. You are just the person I want to see. Excuse me friend. You are not allowed here. This is a restricted zone. And who let you in? Not who, but what you should ask. And pray tell what? Persistence. Persistence? Yes, persistence. Since you are here, what do you want? I have been in the room with the gray tile. Oh, the waiting room. If that is what you call it. It seems like I have been in there for an eternity. Let me check. Hmm. Uh…not quite but the usual amount of time. So, how can I help you or should I say, how can I help you help yourself? The usual double talk. It's all I get around this place. Nobody knowing anything. Everybody with that blank look or look of anxiety. Then the loud speaker goes off. Sometimes one or two. Sometimes 100 or more. It is driving me crazy. Please be patient Mr. Gold. How do you know my name? A trade secret. Now, please return back to the waiting room or…Or what? Please. Be cooperative, Mr. Gold. Some goon is going to come in and straighten me out? A fate that is more awful that you know. Remember, whatever happens will be your own doing. Now please…I am not leaving until you answer some questions. This is highly out of order Mr. Gold. Please. Wait one second…Yes…Yes…I see. Thank you very much. Mr. Gold, I have been instructed to assist you in this matter of yours. It's about time! I always strive until I succeed! So now, where are we at here? And what time is it? And when do I get out of here? Mr. Gold, Mr. Gold, Mr. Gold! Your questions will soon be answered in one quick swoop. You see, Mr. Gold, your situation is quite a common one. The only difference is that we are talking about it. It is highly unusual for this to happen, but it has happened. And dealt with the same way. Dealt with? That sounds if I have caused a major uproar and believe you me, good! Now, deal with it! Now, deal with me! Of course Mr. Gold. We are only too glad to help. Now, you need to go through door number 49 and all your questions will be satisfied. It's about time I see the big cheese. So long, pal. Good bye, Mr. Gold. See you soon – maybe. Nurse, heartbeat? 49 and rising. Good. Very good. Continue with heart massage. I guess it wasn't his time yet. I guess not. Some things in life or near the end of life, we choose life and refuse to go. Or maybe we feel we must turn ourselves around and redeem ourselves for some sin, known or unknown. Who knows? Who knows?

Republicofdos

Greetings my twinqual (twin + equal). Greetings my illustrious twinqual! Twinqual, are you sure of what you just said? My twinqual, I now realize my incorrect verbiage. Greetings my twinqual. That is better. You must remember and must be reminded that we are all equal and that no superlatives are to be uttered. Even words and the way they are conveyed must be plain, ordinary, and equal. Yes. I am sorry. So, the people are content and equal. Is that correct? Yes, my twinqual. Are there any here to speak to me? No. No? What do you mean no? Twinqual, you have just erred of the only law that you have promulgated. That is not so! Again, twice. But…but…but…A mirror shattered and then there was one.

Seaweed

What is this mess? Kelly! Come here, right now! You bellowed? Ha ha! I bellowed! I am unpleased at what I found here. Found where? Found here. Oh there. Yes there. Enough answering questions with questions. With what, dear? With…Enough! Look at this! I can't make heads or tails of this. It's more like a fairy tale from what I can see. I let you run the business as far as the money goes. Everything is straight forward. This comes in. That goes out. Over there stays over there. No shell games. No phony baloney. Nothing below board. Everything on top of the table. Got it? Got it, Sal. Yeah right. This is like the third or fourth time I let you do this stuff And each time, more worse than the last. "Oh please let me help you! I am so bored. I want to be part of your work." You begged me over and over and I did. The result: an unmitigated mess and who knows how long it'll take me to fix this up. I guess I have nothing else to do for the next three or four days. Hello, who's this? Oh, Mac, it's you. What can I help you with today? I see. A number 36 is what you need. You don't think so? You are telling me what to do? Oh! I see. That does complicate things. How 'bout a number 32 with a dash of section two? You're right, Mac. This combo would work much better. It's not something that is normally done but has worked well when implemented. Alright. When do you need it done by? A little earlier than I might be ready. I will give it a shot. Talk to you later. Give my best to the boys. I can always count on them in a pinch. Take it easy. Bye. Kelly, come here. Yes, Sal. I have a call that I must attend to rather urgently. I'll be leaving here in a couple of hours or even sooner if I can I cannot be interrupted on this one. Mac…How is Mac, Sal? Sends his love and looks forward to the club meeting. Now, back to what I was saying. This is an incredibly important job that must be done precisely and correctly. No room for error. Well, there is never room for error but more so this time than others. Remember, no interruptions unless it is an emergency or a call from Jack. Got it? Yes, hun. There we go. Here is the address. Yes, I am…We know who you are. Come this way. Hello, I am…As Lane stated, we know who you are. I am following your instructions implicitly. Thank you for your cooperation. Such a disclosure would jeopardize my good name and that of my family. I understand that completely. It is my policy never to reveal any information regardless of the standing of the family. Absolutely! Lane, take the gentleman to the private drawing room. Yes, Mr. Candi. All done. Thank you for your help and your utter consideration in this matter. You see, Mr. Balone, how would it look if I – the president of the world's largest candy company loved by millions – to have this problem. I agree, Mr. Candi. Hello, Kelly I am home. How did it go? Great. Everything went well. Oh, the phone is ringing. Hullo, Dr. Balone speaking? Cavities are us. How can I help you?

Shadow

Yourself? No, YOURSELF! I don't think so. For what reason? The reason is not for you to know but to engulf, rejoice, and accept the facts as they stand. I cannot do that. You must! Absolute acceptance is the only option available. But that is not a thing to accept blindly. For we are ourselves not some ulterior or forsaken notion that is our past or the given yet unwritten future. It is behind us and we must, yes, understand its presence but not to allow it in as a guide or worst, a hard learned lesson. So, the point of this argument is mute for you: do you accept the existence? You argue from a specious and backward logic that is a cancer in our bones and thorns in our side. And, yes, I accept it as not dictated by my opening words. Then why do you give me a long winded and specious argument? Only for you to choke on fish bones that got passed the monger. My Lord A., you always know how to ruin a good lunch! My Lord P., a good nap!

Sine Die

Ladies and gentlemen, please rise. The court is in session. The Honorable Justice William Smoltz presiding. All please be seated. Are all parties present? Mr. Prosecutor? Yes. Present. Mr. Defense Attorney? Yes, your Honor. Mr. Defense Attorney, is your client present? Yes, your honor present. Very good. Clerk, please note that all interested parties are present and we are ready to call in the jury. Bailiff, you may bring the jury in. The jury please be seated. Ladies and gentleman of the jury the people of this great state thank you for your service for justice and equality. Your open-mindedness will be balanced on the scales of justice blindfolded so only to see the truth. I believe and so the persons present today will appreciate your careful considerations of the facts as presented. Whether you find for the people or for just this one person, you know that you have been fair and equitable. Traits that must be demonstrated so that all may come to the halls of justice to have their wrongs righted and to afflict those guilty of crimes no matter how small nor heinous they may be. This is plainly stated by our forefathers in the establishment of a moral code for this country. Thus implemented fairly by the system of checks and balances as guided through the judicial system. Whatever decisions you or others like you render in courtrooms throughout this state, country, or the world are not and should not be based on a popularity contest or what you hear at the water cooler. But based on the facts those presented you and not a deep seated prejudice toward this one or that. It is a mighty challenge for judges of the fact and judges of the law to sort through hearsay, gobbledygook, and utter nonsense. Accept the facts plainly as given and do not try to interpret or speculate. Leave that to the tabloids or gossip magazines. It is you. It is each one of you who make clear in his or her own mind the sense of the evidence that is given. The sky is green. It is nonsense but you must accept it. Not open to interpretation or discussion. Accept as fact or rule. The rule of law is not open to discussion or its original intent. It is what it is. You cannot say this law is bad or this law did not go far enough. That is for the legislatures and their constituents. This is the final step and great leveler of facts. Remember, no one person is perfect or smarter or knows more than anyone else. Be fair – as I believe you have been and will be. With that said, will the defendant please rise. Mr. Foreperson, have you reached a verdict? Yes, we have your Honor. In the case of The People of the Staten of Olaria versus Thomas E. Wendt, we find the defendant…

Sludge

What is this mess? What have we gotten into? This is horrible. A thick, pea soup, of muck, muck and more muck. A situation that is beyond comprehension. A bleak concoction of a dark, soupy, slime that is only imaginable in a science fiction story or psychological thriller. The black rose. The vampire bat. The black widow spider. The things that just don't bump in the night but the loud thud of your grandmothers' good china. The evil that lurks in everyone's head that we control by the flick of a mental switch. But, in this case it is short and we need a good repairman. Who is this repairman? Where can I find him? Is the answer found in the yellow pages under electrician or under grave digger? Can the answer be found at the local storefront church or the desk of the boss of some multinational corporation? Or can the answer be found on the subway walls or at the foot of a statue? Who knows? A dogs' bark? Who knows what is passed on in the message. Perhaps the answer to a thousand questions or just one is revealed but only known to the great animal gods or the vet. But to our original thought – crap, garbage, oil slick, manure, or anything else you would like to call it. But this is? How do we get ourselves out of this primal goo that was thrust upon us since the first being walked upright and said, "I am." Good. We have made progress, but how much? This is the same primordial slop that still exists today. But the difference is that we call ourselves modern instead of neanderthal. It is a continuing saga of page after page, day after day, week after week, birth after birth, death after death. What are we to do? Continue our existence. Pay out taxes. Go to worship services. And the thousand other things that are repetitive. Go through not having the answer to anything. "What's for breakfast?"

"I don't know?"

"Can you lend me five bucks?"

"I don't know. You never paid me back from last time." And so on and so on. There is only so much time to contemplate these things.

"What are you doing?"

“I am thinking.”

“Thinking, are you?”

“Yes.”

“Well, I’ll tell you what. Pack up your thinking cap and your other cerebral goods and get out. I need a worker not a thinker.” So much for paying taxes and eating. This is getting us nowhere. It’s up to you, you, and the guy behind the tree. It’s your problem. There is only so much we can do. Well Gus, I think we have reached a similar conclusion. We can email the results to corporate. Uh, Mr. Simmons, we thank you very much for your interest in our product however, based on the results from today we can firmly say that we cannot sell you the life insurance from our firm. Perhaps…Oh there is that loud bang again. Drop Simmons down chute number three. I’m glad that was the last one for today. You’re right Buck. This job is starting to get me depressed. You know, you are a real card!

Snowflakes

Herobitus? Yes, my Lord Runius? Come hither. My Lord? What do you see? Physically, emotionally, or spiritually? I have trained you well! I feel confident you will carry on the great strides and traditions of logicality. Thank you, my Lord. But to the question at hand...Physically...I have caught you again, Herobitus! I feel mundane in your presence! Feel not for all things will never be achieved but inferred and speculated against. Yea, My Lord. Yea. I shall tell now what you see! Yes, Runius? You must see the world as it is. The invisible as opposed to the visible. The masks of things are not made up of skin or sackcloth, but shields and armor. Of things that cover and warm. Of things that are a delight to view or touch. Yea, I say, Herobitus, you see them but you too see them with rose colored eyes and slanted thought. What you must do is expunge all that is a filter to what is real, what is not false, what is anathema. Then you see the real truth and intangibles that facade each one of us. I stand before you clothed in drab colors and an unshaved head. Herobitus, again look again! Look and see! Look and touch! Look and divine! Runius...Speak not for I shall pose an interrogatory. See the simple snowflake or raindrop. Both the same but in different forms. Neat and tidy or uneven and random. Which is which My Lord Runius? That is for each one of us to decide. Based on what we see and based on what we perceive. My Lord Runius... my Lord Herobitus... And who is the student and who is the teacher? I have taught YOU well... Okay Vitusis, remove the mirror and you should be ready for all things. Thank you father. Thank you my son.

Squid

Rufus, I think you got a good thing going on here. I think so. I would never have thought you could come up with such a brilliant idea such as this. My mind is awash with all sorts of junk. Junk is the word. Righto! A little junk. A little patience. A little coffee. A little sleep? Nope. Very little of that. Your girlfriend, Jane…You mean my former girlfriend Jane. What happened now? The mad scientist so bottled up in his work that he misses the little things, like friends and more friends? At this rate, less friends and less friends. You better hope I don't get sick and tired of being treated like a third-rate companion. Don't really feel that way. You are my partner, albeit, little hesitantly, but surely coming around. Alright, Ruff, you got me. Thanks, T. NOW BACK TO OUR SHOW! Do we have our list together? Uh, not yet. I am a little hesitant concerning some and too hesitant on others. I understand. This has to be a precise science. There is not much room for error. Rufus, each time I think about it, I get very excited about the concept involved. But the future, the future. The future T? What if this thing gets out of control? I can assure you it will not. I too share your concern, but fret not. If you and I am the only ones involved, why should we worry? Or should I get rid of you, T? Absolutely not! I guess I am just a pessimist. Sorry, I take everything back. Okay. Apology accepted! Now back to our work. Hmm. Hmm. I don't understand your trepidation, T. The list appears to fit the criteria we have established. Which ones cause you grief? Or does your sense of mores not allow for even a minuscule sense of regret?, T. I am a little concerned about your enthusiasm for this project. After all, you were there at the start and encouraged our forward motion. Now, you are concerned? Now I am concerned. I am sorry, Rufus. It is so important that this be near perfect. T., it will never be perfect. Human beings were not meant to perfect but almost always right. I am almost always right. And you can be, too, T. So, let's get on with this thing. I'll strike from our list, just for now, some that are listed here. Okay? Okay! Good. Now, shall we start at the beginning or would you like to throw a dart? No thanks.

T., you make the first choice. How about this one? Let's see. Hey, wait a minute! I appreciate a good joke but this is a little eerie. What is so eerie about it, Rufus? My name. What is it going here? A joke? Right? I am afraid not, Rufus. You said it yourself – no one is perfect. When it comes to human beings, we can be almost perfect. In this case, perfection is not the issue. Judgment. It is all judgment. But who are we to judge the existence of another human being. In a court of law? Perhaps. But a sense of checks and balances must be present in such an environment. And it is. But, in the situation we have or should I say, have let you construct, checks and balances does not exist. Your flawed judgment is acceptable as a human being but not when sitting in a gold throne on the dais of justice. No. No. It is you who are deemed insufficient. It is you who are deemed expendable. It is you who are deemed guilty of wrongs you have committed against the innocent and just. I am the angel on your right shoulder. I am the angel on your left shoulder. I play both sides against your middle. I am the great emancipator of your soul. I pushed you to the limit on one side and hoped you would not spring back. You did not. You failed in your moral choices miserably. You chose the easy over the difficult. You chose to be judge, jury, executioner without ever being the man behind the curtain. You chose wrong. Your name is the only one on the list. It always was and will always be. If not you, someone just like you. And me, I will be there too. Nameless. Faceless. Always present. Always stretching. Always testing. Rufus, your name is up.

Squirrels

Mary…Oh Mary! Stop shouting Sam. I hear you! What's the matter? I was just looking at our accounts and we seem to be spending a little more than usual. Of course you silly! Prices are up everywhere. When I went to the meat market, I was unable to buy the little extra something that we have every week. As a matter of fact, I was barely able to get our usual. Even the chicken cost more. I guess drumsticks will be our sustenance, along with the usual rice and beans. An occasional shrimp or two because I know you love seafood. You're right Mary. It seems like we never quite have enough to get what we really need or want but just enough to get the things that keep us going. I didn't mean to criticize you. I am very sorry. Don't worry Sam. I understand. I really understand. I know it's just not us. I seen Mrs. Williams and her newborn Jessica at the food store and was watching as she chose between baby food and a small side of beef. She was staring very hard at the beef and then stared harder at her little girl and naturally bought the baby food. Hmm. That's awful Mary. I wish we could get more for ourselves and more for others. There's only so much we can do. I know. You know Mary, as I was coming home from work, I noticed the line around the church was longer than usual. So many more people are hurting. So many more than last year. I even noticed a couple of people I know who were let go from my job. Very sad. Very very sad. Yes, it hurts me, too. On the up side Mary, I see we've been cutting back on our electricity. That's good, Sam. Also, I see our water bill is down. Hon, I now try to wash the dishes all at once instead of whenever there's a dirty dish or glass in the sink. A little less water too, in the bath or shorter showers. Mary, you're a great gal, a great mother, and a great wife! I couldn't have done it without you! Thank you, Sam! I couldn't have done it without you either! Ah! What a life! I'm barely home anyway, that's my little contribution. It's not much but at least I can get a free cup of Joe at work to keep me going. You know Sam, you can't be drinking coffee every day. It's no good for you 24/7. Even your doctor says so. All that racing around, without a decent meal is not a good thing. The last thing we need is a medical bill and no income. A salad is easy enough to make. As a matter of fact, I do make a salad for you. Don't you eat it? If you want me to make it differently then let me know and I will. Changing, the subject and returning to the same, why is it that we are still short, Mary? And again I ask, what is it you do with the salad, Sam? Okay you got me and I hope you are not angry with me but...You don't have to explain to me, Mary. I was at the bank across the street and noticed Mrs. Williams hugging you. And you Sam, I was at the nail salon and I saw you getting off the bus in front of the food pantry and...Well, there we are. I guess any extra to us, Sam, is basic to others. Yep. Oh yeah. Hmm. Hmm.

Starless

What a great day! Why do you say that? I don't know. It just is and I feel like the rest of the day will be as good if not better. Lucky you. I embrace your thoughts but I feel the same – but just the opposite. I won't ask you why because you are going to say just what I said about a minute ago. How do you know that? I guess I really don't know. So, let me make it official – Why did you say and feel that way? I don't know. Now we're even. Ugh! So, what are you up to? I thought I would try some mental exercises today. A somewhat bleak day weather-wise but good enough for brain stuff. From what I can tell, physical things would be good, too. We do that, too. But, this is not the time. I think running around a track or 400 sit-ups or push-ups may be good for your body but may be overwhelming to the senses. Sounds like excuses. Sounds to me like your brain is mush. Mush? Yes, mush. Video games and more video games are only good in moderation and to the folks who make them. So is the internet a distraction. This conversation is getting us nowhere. It's getting you nowhere because you can't defend it or at least acknowledge the substance of my argument. Not true. Not true. Really now! You can agree with some I say? Just a bit. I do say mental exercise is a good thing. Keeping the old noodle a lean mean thinking machine is great but playing video and other games also keeps things fluid. Along with the fluids you have while gaming? That has nothing to do with this conversation. Oh really? It's all burned off when I exercise. So, if you don't feel like exercising the beverages you have to kinda' stay put. Right and wrong. In moderation they make little or no difference. But some of the liquids do stay and make a little love fat. Ha! Love fat? Yes, love fat! Whatever. So back to the subject at hand. Your so-called mental exercises. A mental giant? NO. How 'bout a mental welterweight? Now that's closer to the truth! It's starting to rain. Let's get back inside. Okay. Now, where were we? Oh, yes! Perfect conditions. A steady rain. Thunder and lightning about. Conditions perfect. The energy of this earth and of the skies in complete harmony! Oh mother earth! Oh Gaia! Aah! The togetherness of all! The unity of unities! The warmest of the warm! The coldest of the cold! The alive of the alive! The dead of the dead! All bound by a single thread of commonality. The single-mindedness of survival. The spider's thin but strong strand to capture its aliveness. The ability to think – however minutely, however simply, however imperfectly. A sponges' existence. Can it think? Perhaps. Can it function? Yes. Basic functions it has. But can it truly think as we know it? We don't really know or will ever know. But if the gods deem it so they can make a sponge think. I can think. But, can we make use of this thing in a real way? Use it. Manipulate it. Ignore rationality or live by its credos. Think man! Think! Before we all become that primordial slop and slink back into the oceans. Whoa! That was heavy. It was meant to be heavy. Oh by the way, thanks for participating in my little brain exercise. Wha? Yeah, I thought so!

Vulgate

Lots of double-talk from what I can see. Really? Yes really. Concerning what? Concerning everything. How so? Not from just what I can see, but hear and speak. Please elucidate me. Are you that naïve so as not to recognize all this nonsense. Maybe the nonsense you experience is sensible to me and the thousands of others like me. Ridiculous! Now it's ridiculous. Enough bantering and let me make clear some things here. First of all, the translations from Girondic to Belspar are off by so much. Doesn't the fact that Von Bueling – the best in his field – devoted many years of life – to that work that was so intensive it nearly killed him? It makes no difference how intense or the time he took to do his work, it was many day and night wasted based on incorrect premises and faulty calculations. Balderdash! Balderdash yourself! Wrong is just plain wrong. How you continue arguing is beyond me since so many in his field came up with the same conclusions with the same data. Hey look. I can get as many experts as you can and they can reach just the opposite or none at all. Besides, for every one expert you can come up I can come up with five. It is a specialized field. Of course I won't have as many rocket scientists as you do for the very reason I just mentioned. Wrong is wrong and fish stink from the head down and that's it. My stinky fish may be stinky, but there are so few of them and they are in my part of the ocean. Very funny. No, very logical. From a normal point of view, that makes sense. But I can not agree with you any further. To try a different tact. Okay. What is or are the parts you agree with. For one, I agree that Von Bueling is a genius. Normal folks like us don't think that way. Spending twenty-four seven on a project as complicated as his was monumental. But the fact remains – he was and is wrong on the results. Okay, friend. What would you recommend or who would you recommend as somebody who could figure this thing out? I am not sure it can be any one person or any one group or any combination of many a number of people. Perhaps there might be a simpler and less complex answer or even a simpler, more obvious choice to give as a solution. Generations have striven but have been as unsuccessful as Von Bueling but without the enthusiasm or intensity or the near death experience this man has experienced. Therefore, the answer may be as simple and as uncomplicated as one plus one. Tommy, come here. Yes Daddy. Tell Mike how old you are. I am four and a half. And son, what have you been doing today? I was out with mommy and then we came home. I then took a nap and have just finished eating lunch. Sounds like a busy day, Mikey. Yes, it was. I have a question for you. Yes, Daddy? You always ask me questions so I thought I would ask you one. Okay, Daddy. It's the question that you often ask me that I don't have an answer for. Oh, yes, Daddy. That one. Yes, that one. The answer I give you. Do you remember it? Yes. What is it Mikey? Yes, Daddy. The answer is that you don't know. And the question is "why are we here?" Out of the mouth of babes. Yes…babes…babes.

Wisdom

Hey Bill! Hey, Frank you ole' dog you! Fancy seeing you here, Bill. What brings you to the third floor other than your feet? I am here to help you out. Help me out? Don't you remember filling out a Form 92X some time ago? I do. It is a rare occasion that anybody takes notice. Well, someone did and here I am. But how could you be spared? The boys on the twelfth floor are pretty slow these days and felt that sitting around taking bets on the outcomes wasn't something well spent. And how long do I have the pleasure of your company? I was told, Frank, that it is open ended so I brought my lunch just in case. We have our own cafe and food is pretty cheap. Always frugal Frank! That's me. Always trying to save some change. Yep! Okay, Frankie, let me get started. Where is the encasometer control? It use to be where you remember it but was moved to the left side. Smart idea. It was mine, Frank, I feel so privileged to be working with a genius. I know. My modesty forces me not to disagree with you. Alright, Frank. Let me sign in and we can get started. Oh, Bill, it really isn't that busy since I filled out that 92X. I really think I can handle it myself. I am sure, Frank. That you can. However, the penthouse. decided to have one of their big pushes again. Again? Again. But why now? That is never explained or discussed. Only those who need to know know. You and I and everybody else do their bidding. Besides, why should you or I care? Hmm. Alright, here we go. One more thing, Frank. Yes? You are now to use bauble 396 as your master. 396? I never heard of it. Me either. But like I said, do their bidding and don't make waves. Okay. Take 242 out. Put 396 in. Begin. So, what else keeps you busy, Frankie? Once in a while I go and see my mother. How old is she? She is 136. Rather still on the young side. Good genetics and good medicine. Does she speak and is she able to move? Not really. They have her sitting up propped against an overstuffed pillow. An occasional grunt or twitching of the eye. The machine she is hooked up to translates all her electrical impulses to motor activity and an occasional word or two on the neuro-monitor. You know all this stuff, Frank? Yep. I read "Modern Muck" and and just absorb it like a sponge. What about me, Frank? Bill, if you are not smart by now you will never will. Ouch! Double ouch! Oh, by the way, Frank, we have a little surprise for you. Meet, Jaime, my new assistant. What do you mean, your assistant? You see, bauble 396 has only one name in it and it's yours. That is unheard of! You' are right, Frank. It was unheard of up to today. You see, we can not only program forward but reverse it as well. Nothing is wrong with me. Except your modesty, lying and some more lying. You didn't go see your mother. That was a spectral image of her from long ago. She actually passed many years ago at the ripe out old age of 92. All you viewed was a well-worn copy of a copy filmed just after she left us. That is my she didn't move. And when she did, it was with piano wire. So, there it is and there you will follow. I still don't understand. As you can tell, we knew about you for a very long time. So when you did your job, you were selfish and conniving. Frankie, it's time to go. Help him out, Jamie. Now. Let me see. Bauble 46 should work nice. A couple millennium and we should all be back on track. You know, Jamie. Yes, Bill? Those people who pass out brains should be a little more discreet and low-key. Like you, Bill. No, let's say like, like…okay like me!